T0064569

Raven Masquerade;

First Dance

Ren Elmore

authorHOUSE®

AuthorHouse™ LLC
1663 Liberty Drive
Bloomington, IN 47403
www.authorhouse.com
Phone: 1-800-839-8640

Published by AuthorHouse 03/13/2014

ISBN: 978-1-4918-7461-5 (sc)
ISBN: 978-1-4918-7462-2 (e)

Acknowledgments

First, I'd like to say a big thank you to my
husband, David. He's always encouraging me
to do more. Secondly, I'd like to give a big shout out
to my little girl, Gwendolyn. She's one of the major
reasons I strive to be the best I can at everything I do.
I'd also like to say thanks to a very special friend of
mine, Ashley Fitzpatrick, who loves what I write,
regardless of what it is and constantly kept asking for
more of what I wrote. Lastly, I'd like to say thank you
to all my family that believed that
I would get this far in life.
Thank you everyone!

Chapter 1

The world has changed. We no longer associate the differences in humanity. Humanity is us. Outside of us, there is *them*. Creatures of the dark. Demons, werewolves, and vampires. Even the occasional fae. They live with us. But they aren't us. Telling ourselves they don't exist is pointless. They do exist. I've seen them. They need us to survive. We survive with or without them. Some of us have fallen into their services. Some of us are born into servitude. You never know who is, until it's too late. I thought it would never happen to me. I was wrong.

My name is Raya Misten. I'm a petite five foot nothing with hair almost the same shade as the moonlight on a cold winter's night. My eyes are a shade most people call amethyst, but I've seen the gem, and my eyes are more of a neon violet compared to it, as if they actually glow in the light. My heritage makes my skin pale as alabaster in the winter, and a deep golden during the summer. Currently, my skin is a nice creamy color, almost like someone poured milk into a cup of coffee. I'm a second generation psychic. You're probably thinking that puts me with them. No, not really. At least, not fully. A psychic is half of them. I'm half human, a quarter vampire, and a quarter fae, hence my unusual coloration. This makes my powers stronger than most. You'd think the farther from them you go, the weaker the power. Not true. It gets stronger. I have the power to see the future. Most of the time.

Believe me, if someone had told me I'd become a slave, I'd have laughed at them and told them to go fuck off. It was never going to happen. I was too smart to fall so low. And yet, here I am. A slave. Now, you might be wondering what a slave is. It's not what you think. Oh, I'm sure there are masters who treat their slaves as such. But not mine. A slave is a person who has seen their death, and called for help. Called them for help. If the slave is "lucky" their call gets answered. If not, they die without ever becoming a slave. Simple right? Slaves live as long as their masters let them. If the master dies, the slave dies. It's as simple as that.

How did I become a slave? That's not an easy question to answer. Most slaves don't recall their former lives. I do. Boy do I wish I hadn't. I wasn't going to die. I got careless. My mother calls me weak. I had been on my way home from another job interview. I didn't get the job. Something about telling the guy his whole family and him were going to be slaughtered by a rough werewolf on the next full moon not being a job requirement, and therefore disqualified me. I couldn't help it. I felt he needed to know. But, I digress.

I was on my way home from the failed job interview. Without realizing the time, I cut through the park. Nobody goes through the park. Not at night. Didn't realize it was that late. Don't know how I didn't notice. Maybe it had something to do with the fact that the cops had questioned me about the deaths I had told the guy in full detail of how they were going to happen. Again, I digress. Cutting through the park at night is a bad idea. Something could happen. Something did happen.

There I was, minding my own business when I was jumped. Now, most of you are thinking how does that affect me now? Well, I was jumped by them. Four of them in total. Three vampires, and a werewolf. I can smell them. Comes with being a psychic. Two pinned me to the ground, and the other two started ripping my clothing. They were wanting some fun seeing as their last toy broke to easily. Kicking at two of them, and struggling out of the others' grasp, I bolted. I hadn't gotten far when they tackled me again. I had spirit. They liked that.

Kicking again, I got free again. Maybe they were toying with me. I don't know. Reaching the water fountain in the center of the park, I stumbled in. It was lit up, to keep most creatures of the night away. I don't know if it really works. I do know there was a man standing in the middle of it. He helped me up. Demon. I knew it the minute I saw him. The four that were chasing me sensed it too. They stopped outside of the fountain's ring.

"Give us our prey!" and "We saw her first, go get your own!" shot up from them. Without really thinking, I clung to the demon. I'd rather end up with him, then with them. So far, he hadn't tried to feel me up, despite my chest being very visible. He looked at the four of them, then back at me, and smiled.

"Shall I help you?" His voice was calm and gentle. It reminded me of my father's. Looking up at him, I knew I shouldn't accept his offer. I had seen slaves and their masters. But, I wasn't on the brink of death. I was save from being his slave.

"Yes, please help me." The words left my mouth without me realizing it. He smiled again and told me to close my eyes. Nodding my head, I did that, burying my face in his shirt, inhaling his cool crisp scent. He smelled of fresh rain. Behind me, there were screams of agony. After a few minutes the night was silent again. I felt him look down at me, felt his breath against my ear.

"Now, Raya Misten, you are safe." My eyes jerked open. Ripping myself away from him and staring at him. He knew my name. Only a master could do that. I looked at my body, and sure enough, there was a mark above my heart. Twin feathers. Raven feathers. I had been made his slave.

"You can't! I wasn't going to die! I'm not your slave!" I stumbled away from him, slipping on the wet stone. Falling back, he caught me just before my head would have smashed against the fountain's wall.

"I can, and you are. My name is Raven. You don't need to call me master. Just Raven will be fine. Now, Raya, I think we should get you home." He pulled me against him, holding me close. His grip was firm, yet gentle.

"How can I be your slave? I wasn't about to die." I asked, shivering against him. It was cold, despite being summer. He laughed. It sounded almost like rain itself.

"I'm not a lesser demon, Raya. All you had to do was ask for help." He picked me up, and carried me to a car not far from where we were. Setting me inside, and draping a coat over me, he shut the door. A few seconds later, he was in the car with me, and we were on Main Street. He turned up the heat when I shivered.

"If you're not a lesser them, then what are you?" I asked, my body warming up from the heat.

"I'm nobility." He glanced in his rear view mirror, then changed lanes. "And for the record, you're lucky I was there and not my brother. He's been watching for a slave as powerful as you." My heart stopped.

"You're blue blood? And you have a psychotic brother? My day just keeps getting better and better." He laughed again.

"Yes, I'm blue blood. And yes, my brother is psychotic. You're safe, so don't worry." He glanced at me, his eyes seemed to bore into my soul, without me looking back at him. His eyes lingering over my body. Licking his lips, his eyes returned to the road, and slammed on the brakes to avoid hitting the car in front of us at a red light.

"Jesus!" I grabbed the dashboard, my chest free for his eyes to see again. "How about not killing me." I glared at him out of the corner of my eye.

"Sorry. I got distracted." He smiled and shifted in his seat. Sitting back again, covering myself up, I glanced at him. My eyes trailing him. His long hair was in a ponytail and the color of crow feathers, almost shimmering in the traffic light like actual feathers would. He had piercing eyes that were some shade between a silver and the azure of the ocean. A scar trailed his left eye, and the diamond stud in his ear sparkled from the headlights from the car behind us. He wore a black business suit with a white collared shirt under it. Pursing my lips, I found myself slightly attracted to him. Noticing my eyes wandering him, he shifted again, and cleared his throat.

"So, Raya, where do you work?" He was trying for small talk. I wasn't game.

"I'm not playing 20 Questions, Raven." He chuckled.

"Raya, my dear, you can either answer my questions, or I can probe your mind for the answers I seek. As my slave, nothing about you can be hidden from me." He glanced in the mirror again, his eyes froze as his face tensed with anger. "*Crisánt!*" He cursed under his breath. I knew it was a curse, because my father, human that he may be, did speak their language when visiting with my mother's family. I knew a little, but not enough to hold a conversation. "Raya, love, we have unwanted company. Can you stand being dressed like that for a little longer?"

"No, I want to go home." I said hotly. I may not understand enough of their world, but I wasn't going to be dragged into it, slave or no. He smiled.

"Raya, the man that's following us would kill your family without a second thought if he believed it would allow him to claim you. Which he can't have you anyways, since I've already claimed you. But, he's not as nice as me."

"Let me guess, the psychotic brother?" I said, half joking.

"Yes." His one word answer left me stunned. He hadn't been lying about the brother? If he hadn't lied to me about that, then he could be right. If he took me home now, my family could be in grave danger.

"I'd rather not be dressed like this. But I don't have anything else to put on." I said, muttering the last bit to myself.

"I can deal with the clothing." He pulled out a cell, and punched a few buttons then put it to his ear. "Hi, Micha, it's Raven. I need a favor. My love needs a new outfit. Can we borrow one of yours? No, I'll be sure to return. Yes . . . I suppose . . . Micha, I don't have time for this. Yes. Yes. No. Yes. Possibly. No. God, Micha do you really need to know that? Hold on." He turned to me. "What's your bra, dress, and shoe size?"

"I am not having this conversation with you!" I ground out.

"You want clothing? I'm getting you clothing. If you don't tell me, I'll pry." He glared at me, his eyes cold. He would. I knew that.

"42D, size 4, shoe size 7." I muttered, his gaze going back to my chest.

"42D, dear god, did you really say 42? Dress size 4, and shoe size 7." He rattled back into the phone, laughter came from the other side. A female's laughter. Micha was a woman, but not his slave. They couldn't have more than one slave. At least, the lesser couldn't. Maybe blue blood granted you special privileges. "Thanks again, Micha. We'll be there in just a few." He hung up the phone. "42D?" He looked back at me again.

"Yes. Stop saying it. You're making me uncomfortable as it is, having you say it makes it worse." I fidgeted in my seat. I'd had troubles with my bust size since it started growing. They were big. I couldn't do anything about it. "Who's Micha?" He smiled at me.

"My other slave." Blue blood got you privileges.

"I thought you couldn't have more than one."

"Nobility, remember? We're exempt from that rule." He smiled again, he was doing a lot of that, and I hated it.

"Right." I turned to stare out the window.

"Back to what I asked before my brother found us, where do you work?" His eyes on the road, his knuckles going white from his grip on the wheel.

"I don't. I was job hunting." I said, thinking maybe he'd remove his brand now that he knew I wasn't employed. Some masters did that. If their slaves didn't have a steady job, or a place of their own, they dropped them. Not a good thing to happen.

"I see. Schooling?" I inwardly groaned. He was going to know my whole life story by the time we got to Micha's place.

"What about my schooling do you want to know?"

"Everything." Another groan.

"I don't know the daycare, but elementary was Stonewell, middle and high school were at Ventinus Academy, and collage was Primrose Fashion school."

"Fashion school? What major?"

"Everything from marketing to design." I couldn't help but feel proud at that. I had dealt with being an early bird in school practically all my life. In fact, I was 24, and had gotten my highest degree in all forms of the fashion world in little over two years, something that should have been at least two years per degree. I was a smart bird. Too bad I fell off that smart wagon and landed straight in hell. He whistled.

"How old are you?"

"That's rude to ask. 24." I answered, not wanting him to pry.

"I see." He smiled. "You and Micha will get along fine. She's a model. You're a Fashion expert."

"A model?" The name finally rang a bell in my head. "Oh my god! Micha Findation?!?" I stared at him, mouth open. He laughed at my reaction.

"The one and only."

"Oh my god!! Wait, being your slave, that makes us siblings!" He chuckled.

"Rethinking not wanting to be my slave?"

"Maybe. Who else belongs to you?"

"No one."

"So, you're nobility, but have only two slaves?" I perked my eyebrow at him. He shrugged.

"I'm picky." I choke laughed.

"Picky? Sounds like you just have high standards."

"I do."

"And the psychotic brother?" His mouth twitched.

"Has thirteen. And in case you're wondering, you're better off with me. He mistreats his slaves. I don't."

"I see." The car pulled to a stop in front of a four story house that was the color of honeysuckles with vibrant hot pink shutters framing the windows. The porch that led up to the door was grand, almost picturesque with a white whicker garden table and four chairs on the left surrounded by potted plants, and to the right of the porch was a wood swing that looked big enough to easily fit three or four people on it. The fence enclosing the front yard was also, ironically, white. The only thing missing from making this house look like the good old American dream home was a dog house and Fido. Getting out of the car with Raven, and walking to the door, trying not to panic, muttering under my breath.

"Hi, Micha. I'm Raya Misten. I'm your biggest fan, and now I'm your sister slave." Raven was struggling not to burst out laughing as Micha opened the door to her house. Micha was about five foot two, petite, with long chocolate curls for hair with eyes the same chocolate coloring. Her skin looked to be almost a shade of redwood in coloring, and her eyes glittered when she smiled.

"Raven." She nodded her head, her gaze turning to me. "And you are?"

"I'm your biggest fan!" I blurted out, Raven unable to control his laughter anymore as he ushered me in the house. The front door opened to a spacious living room that had walls the shade of moss. The floor was hardwood with a stone grey throw rug in the center. The couch was off white with pillows ranging in color from vibrant forest green to a watery blue. Archways formed doorways to a kitchen straight back, and to another room just off the left, to the right of the room just short of another archway that led into a hallway was a large hardwood staircase that was trimmed in what looked to be gold.

"Micha, this is Raya Misten." Micha stopped at the bottom of the stairs, and turned to us.

"The Raya Misten?" Gazing at me, breathlessly.

"The one and only."

"Wow. Welcome, my sister. Raven, I've got her outfit upstairs." She turned and started upstairs, I followed her, and Raven followed me.

"So, wait, you've heard of me?" Micha stopped short at the top of the stairs, and turned to look down at me.

"What decent model hasn't? You're the fashion prodigy." She turned and led us down the hallway to a room on the left, just short of what looked to be the rest of the sleeping quarters. She opened the door, and flipped on the light. On the bed was a gorgeous midnight blue sequin mini dress with one sleeve. The matching shade blue shoes on the floor near it were at least four inch heels. There was no bra, or underwear anywhere on the bed. Turning back to her, and looking around the room the rest of the way.

"Um, undergarments?" I asked, trying not to be sick at seeing Raven pressing her against the door frame, going to town on her neck, kissing her fast and hard. His one hand pressing her lower body tightly to his, the other teasing her breast.

"Not . . . needed. Oh god! Raven!" She shuddered, I knew from her actions, she had just climaxed from his kiss and touch.

"I'm not wearing this or no undergarments back to my place." I said, blushing and not looking directly at them.

"You're not going back to your parent's place tonight." Raven said, looking at me.

"What?!"

"It's not safe there. You'll stay here til it's safe for you to go back." He said calmly, and he went back to nuzzling Micha.

"I'm not staying here. I'm going home. You can't keep me here." I ground out firmly. Raven stopped his movement, and Micha's eyes frantically moved between Raven and me. Pulling away from Micha, kissing her on the lips again.

"Go along to the bedroom. I'll be there in a bit." He said calmly to her.

"Raven, just remember, she's new. She doesn't know how it works. Please don't hurt my sister." Micha begged him, almost childlike.

"I won't harm her, Micha. You have my word. Now run along. I'll be there soon. I'm just going to talk to your sister." He kissed her again, and turned towards me, taking slow steps. Micha fumbled with the door, before finally managing to shut it. Raven stood in front of me now. He ripped the coat away from me. Instinctively, my arms flew up to my chest. He grabbed them, and held them away from my chest, letting him see me fully. Shoving me on to the bed, and climbing on top of me, pinning my arms to the bed. Pushing me into the bed so I couldn't fight that way either, he leaned in close to me, his breath hot against my face and neck.

"Listen closely Raya. This is the only warning you'll get from me. You are *my* slave. I am *your* master. You will do as I tell you, or you will be severely punished. Just because I'm not my brother, doesn't mean I won't beat you to within an inch of your life. I am protecting you and your family. That's the only reason you'll stay here. Do I make myself perfectly clear?" His eyes had turned from their steel blue coloring to a deep blood red coloring. I had made him very, very angry.

"Yes, master." I spit out. I didn't care if I made him angry. He had pissed me off when he marked me.

"Good. And I told you, it's Raven. You're more than welcome to call your family, and talk to them. I never said you had to cut all ties with them. You just can't go home." He nuzzled my neck, kissing me lightly. I stiffened, my breathing all but stopping. His tongue left a wet trail up to my earlobe, where he took it in his mouth sucking on it lightly. He moaned. Or maybe I moaned. I wasn't sure. He stopped at the sound. Sitting up enough to look in my eyes. His lust filled eyes portrayed the battle in his body. Micha was waiting on him. But I was a new slave. He hadn't tasted me yet. It was obvious he wanted to. I wasn't ready. No way in hell was I ready. But if he wanted it, he was right. I did have his mark. He could force me. All it took was a simple little order. He got up off me, and walked to the door. I slowly sat up as he opened it. Looking back at me, he smiled.

"I won't force myself on you. I'm not my brother, and I take pride in that. Your bathroom is right across the hall from you. Feel free to draw a hot bath. Night wear is in the dresser on the other side of the bed. Micha's clothing might be a bit small around the chest, but until we have time to go shopping for you tomorrow, you'll have to deal with it. Good night, Raya." He started to close the door.

"Wait!" I jumped up, and he stopped, turning back to me.

"Yes?" He prompted me.

"Aren't you supposed to claim me?" He smiled at me.

"I already have."

"No, I mean, claim me, not mark me." His smile disappeared.

"Raya, I told you. I won't force myself on you. I'll wait til you come to me, wanting to be mine, before I claim you." With that, he shut the door, ending our conversation.

Staring at the shut door, and shivering again. I headed across the hall to the bathroom. It was a decent size, not huge, but not small. The tile on the floor was a crisp pale blue that matched the sky on clear days. The ceiling was an off white in coloring. The porcelain sink, tub, and toilet were a cream color. The tub was a Jacuzzi, big enough to easily fit three, maybe four people in it. Turning on the faucet, and finding the right temp, I spied the bubble bath. Taking it and adding three lids worth of the stuff, I went back to my room, and went digging for a night gown. At first, all I could find were sheer ones, or teddies with a little thong that matched. Finally, I found a silk tank and shorts. Grabbing those and heading back to my bath, I shut the water off. Hissing at the heat of the water, I slowly sank into the tub. Leaning back with my eyes closed, relaxing in the hot water. My mind replayed what happened tonight.

Raven said he wouldn't hurt me. He wouldn't force himself on me. But by god, there was a part of me that wanted him to. He was attractive. I was now sisters with Micha Findation, the newest model in the business, and the one that was rising faster than any other had. Maybe this was my fate. I needed my cards. They would help me. They would clear up if this was meant to be, or if I royally fucked up my life. Maybe Raven and Micha could help me get a job? It would be nice. Micha seemed to take a liking to me. Maybe she was tired of being lonely. I didn't have siblings, so I understood loneliness. Raven. His name was that of a bird. But he wasn't bird like at all. He was more of a panther. Agile, fast, and silent.

I shouldn't give him much thought. I really shouldn't. But I couldn't help myself. The more I thought about him, the more I felt I couldn't live without him. I wondered if it was part of the new mark's affect on me. I decided it was. Lying in the hot water, my hands slowly caressed my skin. Touching my breast, and fondling it, I bit my lip. I had dreamed that a man like Raven would sweep me off my feet, and be my prince. Apparently, I got my wish. Just not the way I wanted. My body hummed slightly at the though of his lips against my neck. What those lips would feel like against my breasts. My hand slipped between my legs, teasing myself lightly. My parent's warning about how a master can manipulate a slave without even being in the same room as the slave echoed in my head. My eyes snapped open, groaning.

What was wrong with me?! I was petting myself after just meeting the guy!

Completely disgusted with myself, I stood up from the bath, draining the water, and quickly drying myself off. I slipped into the shorts and pulled the tank on. Raven was right, it was too tight. Scowling, I ripped the stupid thing off, and threw it on the floor of my room. Taking a minute in my disgust and rage, I looked around the room. The walls were a pale pink you'd use for a newborn baby girl, the carpet was white, matching the ceiling. The four poster bed was the color of ebony, as was the rest of the furniture, which stood out against the pastel of the room. My comforter was white with pink rose vines, the silk sheets a matching shade of of pink. Curling up beneath the covers of the bed, inhaling sharply. The sent of lilacs and lavender hit my nose. Almost like the scent of the ones my mom uses. Without meaning to, I quickly fell asleep. Dreams of my family quickly turned to ones of my new master, making love to me. Jolting upright in my bed, about to beat the living hell out of him, and finding myself alone in the room. Deciding it was the heat of the night, I tossed my covers aside. Lying back down, I drifted back to sleep, thankfully, dreamless this time.

Chapter 2

Waking to the smell of eggs and bacon, stretching, I sat up. Looking around the room and finding Raven at the foot of my bed, smiling at me, his eyes lingering on my body.

"Ah!" I covered myself, and threw a pillow at him. "Get out!" He dodged the pillow, still smiling at me.

"Did you know you make such lovely moans in your sleep, my love?" He looked at me, his eyes seemed to glow.

"Liar! Now get out of my room!" I had curled into a ball under the covers to keep him away from me.

"Raya, what makes you think I would lie to you?" Raven's smile faded, as if I had hurt his pride or something.

"Gee, I don't know. Maybe because you're a demon? Or the fact that you never told me that if I asked for your help, I'd be enslaved to you? You ever think of that?" I growled at him. His eyes widened at me. "What? Just figuring out I have a point?"

"Raya, what are you?" He asked, not coming closer, and not smiling.

"I'm half human, quarter vampire, quarter fae. Why?" I answered, knowing the alternative.

"Your eyes, they glow." I blinked. Then I blinked again, not quite believing what he told me.

"They do not." I said, as if to make myself believe it. My mother had told me that if their blood started to strengthen in me, I could gain some traits of her bloodlines. All of their eyes glowed.

"They do, and they are." I bolted from the bed, shoving Raven aside to stare in the vanity. Sure enough, they glowed a pale violet. A sign of the mixing of bloodlines. Violet glow was regardless of the mixture.

"No." I whispered.

"I think it's pretty. Other than foretelling, what can you do?" I turned to look at Raven, covering my chest with my arms.

"I'm a telepath." Pursing my lips, I was determined to go see my parents today.

"Really?" Raven sounded excited. I glared at him.

"Yes, and why do you have to sound so happy about it?" I was obviously not as pleased at my abilities as he was.

"Because it's rare to find a psychic with more than one ability. How can you foretell?"

"I can use blood and animals. Why do you really need to know this?"

"Because I like knowing what my slaves can do. Get dressed. Breakfast is almost ready." He opened the door, and left the room. He didn't try to do anything to me. Not after he saw my eyes glow. Groaning inwardly, I got out an outfit of Micha's and tried it on. Too small.

Taking it back off, I quickly did a light repair to my top, and I put on my clothing from yesterday and headed downstairs.

After a wonderful breakfast of eggs, bacon, and pancakes, Raven kissed Micha passionately on the lips.

"See you after work, Micha." Raven turned to me, and walked over to me. I looked up at him. He held my chin lightly, but firmly, tilting my head slightly. His lips touched mine, first lightly, then firmly. As if I was the only thing in the world to kiss. After a long moment, he broke the kiss. "See you after work, Raya." His voice huskier than it had been with Micha. Glancing at Micha, her face seemed happy, not mad at the length of time he took with me. My eyes focused back on Raven.

"I suppose so. Am I allowed to leave?" Raven stood still, still holding my chin in his hand. His eyes portrayed the battle to stay home and claim his new slave or go to work.

"You can leave. But be sure to be home by dinner." He said slowly, as if debating on giving me the freedom I asked for.

"Thank you." Raven nodded, and headed to the door. "Raven." He turned to look at me.

"Yes, Raya?" He waited, as if hoping I'd ask him to stay.

"Have a good day at work." Raven perked an eyebrow at me and smiled.

"Thank you, Raya. Have a good day at your parent's. Be sure to bring back what you need to stay with us." He left, without waiting for me to respond.

"Bastard." I muttered after he left. Micha turned to me.

"He is not. He cares more about us then most masters do of their slaves." Micha cleared the table the rest of the way, and headed into the kitchen. Great, I had made my sister upset with me.

"I'm going out now. I'll be back in a few hours. I'll fix dinner tonight, if you're fine with it." I waited for a response.

"Sure. Saves me the trouble. Also, I think Raven would like to try your cooking. Have fun sis." She turned, smiling at me. Sis. The word came out of her mouth so easily. I was still trying to swallow the fact that I was a slave, let alone had a new sibling.

Reaching my parents' house, I hesitated outside. I could go right on in. They were home. But, for some odd reason, it felt wrong. Like I should knock, or ring the doorbell. It seemed silly. I turned the door knob, and walked inside the house.

"Mom! Dad! I'm home!" I shut the door behind me. Mom came running from the kitchen, dad from the upstairs.

Mom is five foot six, petite, and surprisingly, got the dark genetics from her fairy heritage, which gave her skin that's a creamy cocoa coloring with hair that was almost as dark a green as the color hunter green. Her eyes where the only thing that didn't match her fairy coloration. They were a deep red, almost the shade of blood.

Dad is six foot eight, stocky, and one hundred percent human. His fair skin made him look Irish or even Scottish, which he was neither. No, dad was pure Norwegian. His hair was a pale blonde with eyes the color of ice. Somehow, when their genetics combined, I came out.

"Raya! You had us worried sick! Where have you been?" My parents wrapped me in their arms, hugging me tightly.

"I was . . . We need to talk." I hugged them back.

"Talk? What's this talk business? Don't tell me you didn't get the job? You were so sure of that one." My mom pulled me into the kitchen, and sat me down in one of our chairs.

"Well, no I didn't get the job, but that isn't what this is about." I said, my mom drowning out my last bit

"Oh Raya! Why not? How could the company be so blind not to hire you." Rolling my eyes, and trying again.

"You know how you keep telling me not to be tricked by someone and become enslaved?" I asked, shifting uncomfortably. This got her attention.

"Yes, why?" She turned to face me as she dried one of our many plates.

"Well . . . Last night. I got attacked in the park, and there was this guy. He helped me." I started, stopping, and trying to not feel so guilty. I truly hadn't known at the time.

"Ok, so where is this knight in shining armor that saved you?" Mom said, picking up another plate.

"He's at work. He's a demon. Mom, whatever you do, don't freak." Mom perked an eyebrow at me, dad picked up his cup of coffee, watching me over his cup.

"Did you get his number? Is he coming over for dinner?" Dad was human. Mom was half vampire, half fae. Of course, they both believed I should have been married by now. Bringing up Raven wasn't going to be easy.

"He's not coming over, no. His name is Raven. He's very nice, and I'm . . . . his slave." I bit my lip at the last. My mom dropped the plate, my dad choked on his coffee.

"How?!?" Mom shrieked at me.

"I asked for help. He's nobility mom! You never told me what happens when it's nobility!" I argued.

"How can you be married off now? You're ruined!" I squared my shoulders and stood up.

"As far as I'm aware of, I can still marry just fine. He hasn't told me I couldn't marry. And I'm still the virgin little girl I was when I left." I stomped out of the kitchen, and upstairs to my room. I could hear the fighting coming from downstairs. Mom and dad had flipped. Mom was worse than dad. She wanted to go and kill Raven. Dad was trying to get her to calm down, and talk to me about the whole thing. She went silent, and I knew the worst was either about to start, or just ended.

Pulling out one of my suitcases, I started to pack my clothing. Stopping when I heard my door open. Without turning around, I knew it was my dad. He was the calm, cool head between my parents. If mom wanted to know something, but was too mad at me to talk, she sent dad to me. It was the way it had always been.

"What's she want?" Dad cringed behind me.

"She wants to know if you're happy, for starts. If this Raven guy is going to be right for you. If you feel safe with him. And a bunch of other things I don't remember." He helped me pack some of my dresses.

"Don't remember, or just refuse to ask?" Looking him dead in the eyes.

"Refuse to ask." He smiled at me, and I cracked up laughing. My dad was the bravest man I knew. He stood up to my mother, even when she threatened to never sleep with him again.

"For the record, I do feel safe with him. I'm not sure if I'm happy, or if he's right for me. I do know I have a sister slave. I've seen her and Raven together. They seem happy. I also know Raven is refusing to claim me." Packing more of my stuff, I felt that my dad was feeling out Raven through my responses. He may have been human, but it always seemed to me like he had more to him than just the human. Like he might be a psychic as well.

"Why doesn't he claim you? It's his right now." Dad shuffled out of my way as I went to the dresser.

"Because he wants me to come to him. To want him. He doesn't believe in taking his rights from me."

"He wants you to be willing. I understand." My cell rang. Checking the name, it was Micha. Don't ask me how she got her number in my cell, or a picture of her for that matter.

"Hello?" I might as well answer. "Hi Micha. Yes? Um, at my parents' still. I guess . . . Let me ask." I pulled the phone from my ear slightly. "Dad, do you guys have plans tonight?"

"Not to my knowledge, why?"

"Micha wants to know if you guys would be up for dinner at our place." Dad smiled.

"Let me go ask your mother. In the mean time, ask what we can do about the furniture in this room." Dad winked at me, and headed out of the room.

"My dad is going to ask my mom. Is there anyway I can have my furniture at the house? No offense meant, yours is lovely and all, but it's not my style. I can? Great." My dad returned.

"Only if it's alright with some of the family coming too. I just got informed they wanted to get together tonight." Nodding my head that I heard him.

"So, if a small chunk of my family came along with my parents, do you think that would be alright? You sure? Alright. I'll go shopping after we get the stuff moved. Oh? That works. Alright. See you soon." I hung up.

"Micha says she's fine with it, Raven won't mind. And she's sending a couple of butlers to help you move the furniture so she and I can go shopping." Dad nodded his head.

"Alright, just please, change clothes first. I'll leave you be for a while." Dad left the room, shutting the door.

Biting my lip, I pulled out a jean skirt, an ice blue halter top, and a white thong. Getting dressed quickly, I poked around the foot of my bed, finding my platform sandals and put them on. Putting more clothes and other things in boxes and bags. I had planned on moving out soon. A friend was going to let me crash at her place after I got a job. Hearing the doorbell ring, I headed downstairs and opened the door. Standing outside was Micha and two males the size of pro football players.

"Hi Micha. Welcome to my old place." I stood aside for her and the guys to enter. She swept past me barely listening to me.

"This place is so cute!" She squealed at the interior of it. She was wearing a pale pink sun-dress and a pair of white high heels. The bottom of her dress reminded me roughly of ballerina tutus. But that was the current style. Adorable. It was the only thing I could think of to call her outfit. My mom came out of the kitchen, still mad at me, and glared at the new people in her house.

"Well? Introduce us." She ground out. Micha looked at her, and then back to me, perking an eyebrow. I winced.

"Mom, dad, this is Micha Findation. She's my new sister. These guys behind us, are going to help dad relocate my things so Micha and I can go shopping for dinner." I did the best I could, not trying to be too shy of the fact that my mom was still mad at me. Mom glared at my chest. Looking down, I saw why. Raven's mark was visible. I bit my lip, then licked them. She was going to start.

"Why do you have to show your tramp stamp?" She said flatly. Micha's eyes widened beyond belief.

"Tramp stamp?" She repeated and looked at my mom like being Raven's slave was the best thing on earth.

"Yes, that's what I said." My mom glared at her like it was her fault that I was in this mess.

"I don't understand. How can you not be happy for her? Raven's the best!" She smiled.

"Raven is still the bastard that controlled her decision." My mother wasn't going to give up on this.

"Mom, I'm fine. Really." I looked at the floor, tears in my eyes. Micha noticed and wrapped her arms around me.

"How dare you insult Raven! How dare you make Raya feel like all this is her fault! She was attacked! Now, I'm not proud that Raven marked her. Don't get me wrong Raya, I've be asking for a sister for awhile now. But Raven didn't go to the park to mark her on purpose. He was supposed to be meeting someone. Raya happened across him before that man showed. And to protect Raya further, he left before the man showed. He knew Raya would be in more danger if he stayed." My mind went into shock. Raven had kept a man from seeing me? Was it his brother?

"Oh really? Then why doesn't he return my daughter to me?" Micha went white as a ghost, her nails digging into my skin.

"You don't want that. A slave released from their master is as good as dead. They can fall lower than even impoverished people. They fall so low, they don't care who makes them feel alive again. They'll take anything, anyone, to make them feel wanted again." Micha's voice was a harsh whisper. I touched her hand.

"Micha." Her head snapped to me, her eyes lost, as if remembering. "I'm here, sister. You're safe. Raven will take care of us." I smiled sweetly at her. I knew, somehow, this is what she needed most right now. A motion out of the corner of my eye caught my attention. One of the 'butlers' had pulled out a cell, and turned to make a call. Raven's crisp voice came over the phone.

"Sir, we got a small problem. It's Micha. Yes. I understand. Will do. Hm? Raya?" He glanced at me, then turned back to his call. "Yes, Raya's with her. Oh? I understand. Of course. As you wish, Master Raven." Raven's chuckle about being just Raven came from the other end as they hung up.

"Micha's just fine, Brutis." I glared at him. He shuffled a bit.

"How'd you know my name? I don't recall saying it." He eyed me suspiciously.

"I heard Raven call you that. I have very good hearing." I almost growled at the poor guy. The sweat on his brow made me wonder who he was suddenly more scared of, me or Raven. Micha seemed back to normal now.

"I'm fine, Brutis. Really. Raya here helped me." She hugged me tightly. Micha may have been older than me, but I was defiantly the big sister in this situation. I'd have to ask Raven about how she knows so much about slaves.

"Whatever. He'll be at dinner tonight?" Mom waved what Micha said under the bus. If Micha noticed, she didn't show it.

"Yes, mom. He'll be there. You can meet him tonight. How many people will be there?" I thought of my options for dinner.

"Twenty-three." She smiled at me. I coughed.

"Twenty-three?! God, that's what, you guys, at least two sets of uncles and their families."

"The people coming are us. Scott and Juliet and their two kids. Kira and Emily and their little girl. Josh and Margaret and their three angelic brats. Spencer and Tio and their new addition. Lia and Sara and their two kids. Last but not least, Grandpa Larry and Grandma Constantina." Mom got a glare from dad at the mention of Uncle Josh's kids. But, to be fair, they were brats. Groaning inwardly I nodded my head.

"So, aim for a slight vegetarian dinner. Got it. Oh, and some vegan for Aunt Lia. Got it." Biting my lip, I tried to think of what I could do for everyone. Lamb. It wouldn't work for the vegetarian or vegan, but it would be for everyone else. "Lamb work? I know, I know, not for Lia and the others, but I can fix something for them." Mom nodded her head.

"Kay. Well, I'm sure Brutis and his friend will let you know where the house is. See you guys later." I led Micha back out of the house, and found a bright yellow BMW Z4 sDrive35i with a cream interior. Micha got in the drivers side, and I climbed in.

"Wow." She smiled at me. "Expensive." Her smile grew.

"Raven got it for me. If you ask, I'm sure he'll get you a car too." She backed out of the driveway and headed to the grocery store. The all health nuts only food store.

I could tell this was going to be a very expensive trip. Lamb at a normal grocery store was anywhere between thirty dollars to forty. Sometimes even fifty.

"At what cost? And you don't have to go spend several hundred on dinner. We can go to the general store for dinner." I said looking at her. She laughed.

"Maybe, but the general store doesn't have vegan and vegetarian approved lamb. As for the cost, it's simple. Just don't get pulled over, or in an accident." Smiling back at her.

"That's because you already go to him. I'm not ready." My smile faded and she laughed.

"Actually, before he and I ever got intimate he got me the car. I needed a vehicle for work. And I wanted my independence. He got me this." My eyebrow perked at that.

"Really? So, I could ask for my own ride? And he wouldn't ask me to sleep with him for it?" Micha licked her lips.

"In case you haven't noticed, sis, Raven tends to want us to go to him. Not the other way around." I thought about that for a minute.

"How did you and Raven meet?" She glanced at me then back to the road.

"I don't want to talk about it. Let's just say, I've been on the dark side of the masters/slaves side of the world. Raven found me, and brought me back to the light." I nodded my head. It was good enough for me. If Micha ever wished to share, I was willing to listen.

"Ok. So, what's our dinner allowance?" I sat back in the car, enjoying the wind in my face.

"Whatever we need for a smashing dinner." Micha took on a British accent, and I laughed. "Seriously, I don't know anyone with that much family." She shook her head.

"Yeah. My dad's side. He's one of, I think, six." Micha whistled. "Yeah, you should see my mom's side. Then again, we'd be spending over a thousand on food tonight if they were all coming." Micha whistled again.

"That many?" I nodded.

"Most are vampires or fae though, so at least, they're easy to feed." Micha nodded her head, parking the car.

"Alright. Time to go shop." She smiled at me as we got out of the car.

Heading inside the store, I was floored at how much the prices were. The lamb we were needing was one hundred fifty dollars! And that was before tax! They were insane. But, I put three large rack of lamb into the cart, grabbed several cases of booze, some spices, potatoes, onions, carrots, and several other veggies and fruits. At the counter, our dinner grand total was just shy of one thousand dollars. My eyes must have bugged out of my head, because Micha laughed, explaining I shop at the general store.

"Micha, this is how much my household spends a month on food!" I was still stunned at the price as we headed out to the car. So stunned I didn't notice a group of drop-outs from my high school hanging by our car. They didn't miss me though.

"Hey, lookie here boys!" The redhead said. I stopped dead in my tracks. Micha stopped just short behind me.

"What's up sis?" She stepped next to me.

"Randy Davis." I jutted my chin at him. The guy had harassed me all my days at high school. Randy had bright red hair the color of fire, with deep green eyes that almost matched a forest green in shade. His skin was sickly pale, like he'd been ill for most of his life. He had a nose ring piercing, snake bite piercing, most of his left ear pierced, and a tribal dragon tattoo that snaked it's way up his left arm. The tattoo was still fresh in my memory from the time I was in high school with him. He should have been kicked out, but no, our headmaster had wanted to try and 'reform' the problematic youth.

"Randy Davis? Someone you knew from school?" She smiled at me.

"Yeah, not the nice guy type either." I scowled at him.

"Raya, you scorch my heart with that comment. I just wanted ya to loosen up a bit." He smiled at us, his nose ring making me want to rip it out of his nose.

"Right, by trying to rape me in the gym everyday after school." I growled at him. Micha eyebrows raised.

"Aw, Raya. You say it like I was really gonna do it. Come on. You know me better." Randy walked towards me, grinning.

"Get your goons away from our car and go piss off." I wasn't going to let Randy scare me anymore. He'd traumatized me enough when I younger. He wasn't going to ruin my day.

"Your car?" He sounded shocked that it was our ride.

"My car actually." Micha smiled at him. He glanced at Micha, looking her up and down.

"Well, aren't you something else." He smiled at her.

"Thanks, and I'm taken." She walked past him. I followed at his stunned look on his face. Unfortunately, he got better as I pasted him. He grabbed me from behind.

"Ah! Let go, Randy!" Micha turned around, and went to help me, but Randy's goons grabbed her as soon as she tried it.

"Let me go!" She struggled against them.

"Randy, I swear to God, you let me go." He chuckled, grabbing my chest and twisting it hard. "AHH! That hurts!"

"Aw Raya, you're making such wonderful screams." He licked my ear. Hitting him hard with my foot, I got semi free. He re-grabbed my arms and twisted them harder than before.

"AHH!" CRACK! "AHHH!!!" I screamed, my eyes moist with tears. He'd broken my arm. He was stronger than I remembered. Tossing me against the car, I turned a bit to look at him. When my eyes landed on his neck, they widened. Either he had gotten a new tattoo of a snake head, or he was a slave. That explained it.

"Like the new mark? I got permission from my master to claim a woman I want. Up until just a bit ago, I didn't have anyone in mind. Raya, you just made the top of my charts." I shook my head slowly. I didn't care if a portion of my underwear was visible in my current position. He scared me. I was never going to get away from him. Looking over at Micha, she was in just as much trouble. Everyone in the parking lot was ignoring us. They knew better. Randy was bad news. You don't mess with him.

"So, Raya, are you going to keep fighting me with that arm of yours? I'd hate to break your other one." He licked his lips. I shook my head again and threw my good arm up to protect myself.

"RAVEN!!" I heard Micha scream. Only, it wasn't Micha's voice. Everything went dark. Looking around there were feathers falling around me. They turned into a tornado. When they burst apart, Raven was standing between me and Randy. "Raven?" My voice didn't sound like mine. He turned to look at me, and smiled.

"Raya, I see you figured out how to summon me when you need me most." I slowly stood up, cradling my arm. He stepped closer to me, and held his hand out to me. "What happened Raya?"

"Randy and his goons jumped us when we left the store." I dried my tears. Raven would protect us. He would. Raven turned to Randy.

"You hurt Raya?" He asked, not that he didn't believe me. He wanted him to say it himself.

"No way. I was helping her with her bags, and she fell." He smiled at Raven. He thought being someone's slave would protect him from Raven. Raven looked at Micha. She had been released and was putting groceries in the car. He looked back at Randy.

"I see. It seems fair odd that Raya would have lost her balance so badly as to break a limb when she fell." Randy seemed to sweat.

"I'm telling you the truth." He confirmed his own lie to himself.

"Raven, he's lying." I whispered. Raven turned to me.

"I'm well aware of that. You wouldn't have called me if he had been helping you." Raven turned back to Randy.

"I suggest you forget about Raya." Raven was polite, but deadly with his words.

"Hmpf. Dratis!" Randy looked over his shoulder. A man appeared in a similar fashion Raven had. His short hair was spiky and platinum blonde in coloring, his eyes were a green mix of shamrock and hunter green with flecks of lime green in them. He wore a black shirt that had graffiti writing all over it, a white zipper jacket over it, a pair of army cargo pants, and a pair of jungle Nikes. His left eyebrow was pierced along with his both ears, from cartilage to earlobe.

"Yes, Randy?" Dratis smiled at him. Randy nodded his head at me and Raven.

"You said I could take a woman as my own. He's stopping me from the woman I want." Dratis' smile faded a bit.

"I see. Hello Raven. It's been awhile." He walked forward, hand extended.

"Dratis. How has your family been?" Raven took his hand, shaking it slowly. Dratis snorted and shook his head, laughing.

"God Raven. It's been what, ten years?"

"Twenty actually." Dratis nodded his head.

"Twenty. God has it been that long?"

"Afraid so. Ever since your father broke that vase." Dratis smiled again.

"Yeah, and since your mother spread them for my dad." Raven was clearly pissed at this.

"Well, I'd appreciate it if you kept your slaves from mine." Dratis' brow furrowed.

"She's yours?" He looked at me, found the mark, and nodded his head. "Sure. Say, you going to be at Tȩmina this year?" Raven seemed to stiffen.

"I'm afraid I won't be going this year." He sounded almost strained. Like he wanted to go, but was denying himself the pleasure of going.

"That's too bad. I was looking forward to a trade." Dratis looked away from us.

"Oh? That's rare for you. I wouldn't be trading either of my slaves, so I'm not sure what you'd be asking for in return." Raven's voice was genuinely shocked.

"Money. Mostly. Refuge would be nice. But mostly money. Not that I don't have enough, but you can never have too much. A dip in your library would be a good thing too." Raven twitched.

"Dratis, you know the way I feel about the library."

"Yeah, I know. At least think on it?" Raven sighed.

"Fine. I'll tell you what. If, if mind you, I go to Tẹmina, I'll think about your offer." Dratis nodded his head.

"That's good enough for me. Well, I'll hopefully be seeing you, Raven. Come on Randy, you're bothering this man." Dratis grabbed him by the throat and dragged him a few feet away, and disappeared.

"Tẹmina?" I looked at Raven.

"Mating season. Don't worry about it, Raya. We're not going. I'll see you home later. Your arm is fine now." He smiled at me, and I tried to move it, and he was right. It was healed.

"Wow." He chuckled.

"Being a slave enables you to heal almost instantly. Unfortunately, it doesn't stop pain. I'm sorry he hurt you."

"You could have hurt him back though, right?" I looked up at Raven, not wanting it, but wondering if it was possible. Raven gave me a weak smile.

"It's not a good thing to do. If he hadn't been owned, I could have marked him. At which point, I could have done anything in the world to him. And believe, he would have wished he'd never been born. I normally wouldn't mark someone, then drop them. But, for my girls, I would make an exception to anyone who would hurt them. But, off topic, why did you buy so many groceries?" I flinched.

"My family is coming over for dinner. Twenty-three of them." Raven nodded his head.

"Alright. I'll be sure to be home early enough to greet them." He smiled at me again. "I better head back to work." He disappeared.

"Crap." I sat in the car as Micha got in.

"What's up?" She looked at me confused.

"I forgot to ask if he could help me get a job." Micha giggled.

"You'll start work the day after you're settled in." I looked at her. "He got you a job at his company. No worries. You'll enjoy it." She winked at me, and took off.

"How can you be sure I'll enjoy it?" I asked, skeptically.

"Because he works in the fashion industry. I don't know what you'll be doing exactly, but I'm sure it'll be to your strong suit." I nodded my head.

Chapter 3

By the time Raven got home from work, I had two minor meltdowns while working on dinner. The first, caused by the massive amount of mouths I was going to have to feed. Twenty-six mouths was a lot. Working on dinner, I had a whole new respect and awe for restaurant chiefs. They had to deal with way more than just twenty-six mouths a night. The second, caused by Tęmina, their mating season. Why couldn't Raven go if he wanted to? I had found out, that he could go. But, we'd have to go with him. And, we would be expected to perform. When I almost asked what she meant by that, she gave me a knowing look. That kind of perform! No way in hell was I going to have sex with Raven at some place that wasn't home, or in front of thousands of people! Not now, not ever was I going to do that. If Raven and Micha wanted to go, that was fine with me. I'd man the house.

"Can't just you and Raven go? I'll watch the house for you guys." I smiled at her, hoping that was a possibility. Micha giggled.

"As much as I'd like to take you up on that offer, if Raven goes, all of his slaves have to go as well." She finished working on the potato salad and switched gears to get the green beans started. A car door slammed shut from outside. Micha squealed. "He's home!" She dried her hands off, and dashed to the entry way to greet him. I shook my head. She was like a newlywed. Turning back to the lamb I was putting the finishing touches on, a thought struck home. I was sort of like a newlywed myself. I had just moved into a man's house, that up until last night, I'd never met. Ok, that sounded so much less romantic than the thought of Micha as a newlywed, but yeah, I guess in a way, I was. Finishing the lamb, I wiped my hands off, and headed to the same location.

I got to the living room just in time to see Micha hanging off Raven, kissing him like he'd been gone for ages. Stopping short, it felt wrong to watch them. Turning on my heel, I headed back to the kitchen. If he noticed, I'd tell him I forgot to check something. He noticed.

"Raya?" I heard him calling me from the entry way. "Micha, you don't have to cling to me. I'm home now. Raya?" His voice was closer now. Bending down to check on the pie in the oven, I was trying to ignore Raven. It felt awkward to be in the same house as him. Satisfied with the way the pie was looking, I stood up. Turning around Raven was right behind me, making me jump.

"Raya, why did you ignore me?" Looking up at him, his face looked pained.

"Because I had to check the pie. And thank you for giving me a heart attack." I watched his expressions. His face remained the same.

"Raya, do you feel uncomfortable in my house?" He asked slowly. Micha froze over the green beans, as if waiting to hear my response. Depending on my answer, she could feel insulted, or unwanted.

"In a way, yes." I answered slowly. His eyes darkened a little.

"How so?" I hesitated. I didn't want to tell him the real reason. That I felt like a third wheel. I didn't feel like I belonged. Uneasy, I licked my lips.

"I sort of feel like a third wheel." I whispered, tears burning the back of my eyes. I didn't know why I wanted to cry. Was I really sad at feeling like a third wheel in this house? Raven's eyes softened.

"I'm sorry you feel that way. Micha's used to it being just us. I'll make sure to spend some time, just the two of us, after dinner." My heart skipped a beat. That wasn't what I wanted. Was it? The doorbell rang. Raven turned to Micha. "Please get the door, Micha."

"Kay." She left the room. Raven turned back to me, and bent down. His lips brushed mine lightly, pressing a little firmer than this morning's first brush with them. The voices from the entry way snapped me out of the kiss.

"So, where is my daughter?" Pushing against Raven, and heading towards the doorway. Ramming my side into the table corner in my rush, ignoring it, I met my mom just short of the kitchen doorway.

"Hi mom, dad! I hope you guys had a safe trip." My smile somewhat faked. My side hurt. My mom glanced over my shoulder at Raven. I chanced a glance, to find him about to sneak some food. Twirling around to him. "Don't you dare!" He froze, slowly turning to look at me. His expression was that of a canary that just spied the cat.

"Yes, Raya?" He croaked out.

"Back away from the food. You don't get special treatment just because you're my master! You'll wait to taste it with everyone else that's coming for dinner. And if you think for a second you can sneak something without my noticing, you will regret it." He stood upright, smirked at me with a raised eyebrow.

"I will, will I? I'd love to know what you'll do to me." He walked over to the fridge and pulled out a bottled water. Turning back to me and my parents he walked over and extended a hand. "Hello. I'm Raven. Glad you could make it out here for dinner tonight." He smiled at my parents as I walked back to my work space.

"Dierda Misten." My mother took his hand, thinking to shake his, but he put her hand to his lips, lightly kissing it.

"A pleasure, Dierda." He smiled as she yanked her hand back. My dad chuckled.

"Robin." He extended his hand. Raven shook his.

"Pleasure to meet you as well, Robin." He turned back to my mother. "Well, it's plain to see where Raya gets her beauty. Are all Misten women as lovely as you and your daughter?" My mother blushed, not knowing if she should enjoy the compliment, or smack him for it. My dad chuckled again.

"Most of them are." My mother glared at my dad. "They are." He chided her.

"Tell me, Raven, do you always eat in your business clothing?" My mother was searching for what she considered flaws. A workaholic was a flaw.

"No, ma'am. I just haven't had a chance to change yet. I just got home myself." He smiled at her. "But, if you don't mind me disappearing for but a moment, I'll be back dressed for dinner." She nodded her head, to which he tipped his in response, and headed to the staircase. Disappearing upstairs, my mother walked over to me.

"Something smells good. You're cooking. That's a first." She went and sat down at a clear space of the table, my father walked over to the fridge.

"Care if I raid?" He looked at me.

"Go ahead." I nodded my head. "Help yourself." He turned around and checked out the drink selection.

"My god!" He came up for air after a few minutes, holding up a beer. "You can't even get this brand in America anymore! It's all gotta be special imported." He turned to me. "What does Raven do to get the good stuff in his house?" I started to answer, but Raven popped back into the kitchen at that moment. He was wearing a black fitted t-shirt, blue jeans, and a pair of sneakers.

"Simple, some of my best clients deal with the importing of goods. Such as beer. They usually snag me a case of something I show interest in. If you think that's some good stuff, I've got several bottles of a rare wine from the Fae country. Most of this particular stuff never leaves." My mother eyed him.

"Let me see, if you don't mind." She smiled, but I knew what she was up to. Drinking was fine, if you drank the good stuff. Drinking watered down was a flaw, and drinking too much was a flaw. God, it was like she was judging a prospective husband for me. My eyes started darting between Raven and my mother. Was she? Was she expecting Raven to pop the question? He was my master, not my boyfriend. Raven handed her a bottle that I knew was written in the Fae language. Checking the bottle over thoroughly, she determined that without tasting, she could be almost certain it was real. If she could taste it, it would fully pass or fail. Raven got out a bottle opener, and popped open the bottle, pouring her a small glass. After smelling it, and testing the taste of it, she smiled. It passed. I let out the breath I hadn't known I was holding, and all eyes turned to me. Blushing I turned back to my work. Micha giggled, and Raven suggested they head to where dinner was going to be, so as to not disturb our hard work.

"When will the rest of the family be showing?" I asked before they left the room fully.

"In about twenty minutes they should be here." My dad checked his watch. I nodded.

"Good. Dinner will be ready about that time too." Turning back to my work.

Micha watched me as I finished the last few minor details.

"You seem a little tense, sis." Micha rubbed my shoulders a bit after I was done.

"Do I?"

"Mm hmm."

"Maybe I wouldn't be if my mother would stop judging Raven like she would a prospective husband for me." Micha giggled.

"Oh, Raya, don't be silly. If she gives Raven her blessing, meaning as a husband, but not specifying, Raven can take it like he's been given permission to be your master." I hadn't thought of that. Nodding my head, and turning to face Micha.

"Let's go sit with the rest of them while we wait." I smiled at her. She nodded and took my hand. As we headed towards the room, the doorbell rang. Raven turned to look at us. I smile and nudged Micha into the room.

"I'll get it." I headed to the door.

"Hey, glad you could . . . make it?" Opening the door to Dratis and a man I had never seen before hadn't been what I expected. The man was tall, not quite reaching six foot, bald, and stocky. His eyes were a deep brown that almost looked black, and he wore a brown business suit with a slightly rumpled white shirt under it.

"Why thank you, Raya. See, Cain, I told you Raven had a new slave." Dratis turned and smiled at the man next to him. He blinked then turned to Dratis.

"You did? No you didn't. Wait, you did, I remember now. No I don't. Why don't I remember you saying that? You did say that didn't you?" He looked overly confused. He had just convinced himself that Dratis had never informed him about him. Dratis rolled his eyes and sighed.

"Yes I did, Cain. I told you earlier today. You were the one that suggested we come over and introduce ourselves properly."

"I did, didn't I?" He perked up, as if he recalled saying that.

"Mm hmm." Dratis smiled at me. The rest of my family was walking to up the driveway to the house as well. Stepping out of the way, I welcomed everyone inside.

"Everyone, it's good to see you all. Welcome to my new home." I kept a happy face on, and lead everyone to the dining room.

"Raven, everyone's here." He greeted everyone individually, kissing female hands, shaking the males. When he was done, he turned to my father.

"Robin, I believe you told a white lie earlier." My dad's eyebrows raised.

"I did?" He looked a little confused.

"Yes, you told me most of the women in your family were beauties. When, in fact, all the women in your family are beauties." Raven smiled, as my dad chuckled.

"You found me out, Raven. Very clever of you." Dratis and Cain stepped into the room, the last to show themselves.

"Raven, I don't think you've greeted us yet." Dratis smiled at him, winking at me. Raven turned slowly to face the last two to enter the room.

"Dratis. Cain." The second man's name dripped with poison.

"Evening. It's been awhile, hasn't it brother?" Cain seemed completely sane. Micha and I stiffened. Cain was Raven's brother?

"I'm . . . I'm sorry Raven." I stammered, heading to the kitchen for extra plates. Before I could leave, a hand grabbed my throat and held me against something. My eyes rolled to see who. It was Cain. Dratis was ignoring the incident.

"Cain!" Raven almost roared at him. Cain looked from me to Raven.

"Beautiful. Raven why is it you always get the good ones? I'm stuck with incompetent worthless imbeciles and you get the lovely ones." Cain's other hand traced my face slightly. His sharp finger nails leaving little cuts where little pools of red dotted my skin.

"Cain you will release Raya this minute, or so help me god I will kill you here and now." Raven's voice was a whisper.

"I don't think I will just yet. I haven't tasted her." He pulled my face up, and slowly bent his head down to kiss me. The next thing I knew, I was on the floor, supported by Dratis on one side and Micha on the other, and Raven had Cain pinned against the wall.

"If you ever touch Raya again, I will kill you. You've overstepped your boundaries, brother. Make no mistake, I will kill you." Raven growled at Cain. Cain laughed at Raven's words.

"Right, like you said you'd kill Father if he ever touched Micha again? You have no bone in you that would kill Raven. All you are, is a bunch of empty promises." Raven slammed him into the wall again.

"Don't you dare bring that bastard into this. I will not tolerate anyone touching my girls in anyway I don't approve of. And mark my words, Cain. Brother or no, I will kill you if you ever touch Raya, or Micha, again." Raven threw him toward the door of the house. "Now get your filthy ass out of my house!" Cain stood up, laughing as he disappeared.

"You alright, Raya?" Dratis looked at me like was actually worried.

"Yeah, I'm fine." I pulled myself away from Dratis, and stood up. Everyone in the room had watched the whole thing. I was worried about Raven. I walked over to him and touched his arm, his head jerked to look at me. The glow fading from his eyes. "Raven, are you alright?" He looked taken aback.

"Raya, I'm fine. But are you alright?" Raven grabbed my upper arms, firmly, but not hard enough to harm me.

"I'm fine. A little shaken, but otherwise fine." Raven pulled me into a tight embrace, flattening my hair.

"I'm sorry Raya. If I'd known he would have been with Dratis, I never would have invited him. I'm so sorry." Raven's breath was shaky. "You!" He now turned on Dratis, who was heading to his seat at the table.

"Me?" He pointed at himself, apparently unsure of how he got dragged into Raven's shit list.

"What the hell was he doing with you? You know he's not welcome in my house!" Dratis sat in his seat.

"Yeah, I knew that. But it's not like I could have brought my slave with me. He broke her arm remember? I wasn't going to risk him pulling another stupid stunt. By the way, Raya, how is the arm doing? Healed up nicely?" He winked at me.

"Yes, thank you for asking." I replied, most of which was drowned out by Raven's voice.

"Don't you go being nice and cute with Raya! It was because of your dumb slave that her arm was broke! And it's your fault that bastard was here! You almost cost me Raya!" My mom's eyes widened.

"Raya, when was your arm broke?" I groaned inwardly.

"Earlier today. It's fine now. Slave healing does wonders." Turning to Raven. "Wait, you said his stunt almost cost you me. How?" Dratis' laughter roared from across the room causing me to look at him.

"See, love, it's like this. If Cain were to be intimate with you before you were claimed by Raven, Raven's mark would vanish. You'd become Cain's. For the record, kissing is very intimate." I looked up at Raven, who clearly wanted to kill every member of his family at this point.

"Is that true?" I asked, quietly holding onto his arm.

"Yes." Raven turned from me to the rest of the room, taking on a welcoming air again. "Please excuse the display from just a bit ago. My family tends to have issues with acceptance. I hope we can go about the evening friendly with one another." The room echoed approval of the apology, and went about their talk as we got to the table and sat in our spots.

Conversations rose and fell throughout dinner. Everyone seemed to accept Raven and Micha as part of the family. Which meant wonders for them. But I wasn't sure about where that put me. I still wasn't sure if I wanted Raven as my master, or my lover. But, I supposed, seeing his brother, he was the better option. During desert, the talk faded into nothing but compliments.

"So, Raven, what are your intentions for my daughter?" My mother took another drink of her wine, eying us for signs of something. Raven took another drink of his water before answering.

"Diedra, my intentions for Raya are the purest you'll ever find. I wish to help her with her career, see to it that she grows from the beautiful young adult that she is into the gorgeous woman she was meant to be, and to be there for her whenever she needs a safe place to wait out the storm that is life." My mother nodded her head. His answer was very poetic. But, even I knew that wasn't what she meant by her question.

"That's all very nice and caring. But, what of her purity in more intimate relations?" My mother was politely asking her if he intended to be my lover. God bless parents.

"Mother!" I hissed at her. The whole family didn't need to know that kind of thing.

"Raya, it's fine." Raven didn't get the reason behind my desire for her not to be told. "Diedra, my intentions in that ray of light are" He paused for a minute. "Very sensational, yet pure. I will not take part of the baser needs without her consent. As she has not yet given it to me, she remains untouched. And will do so by any male." That last bit was directed at Dratis. He looked shocked at Raven.

"Cousin, when have I ever touched something that belonged to you without your permission?" Fake stunned. Even I could tell.

"Twenty years ago, at Tęmina. You tried to take Micha." Raven smiled, almost threateningly. Just then, My Darkest Days' Casual Sex chorus rang throughout the room. Grabbing my cell out of my pocket as quickly as I could and answering it.

"Hello? Chris, hi! Hm? I guess. Yeah. Tomorrow works for me. Porchino's? Yeah. Alright. I'll see you at seven. Bye." I hung up. Looking around the table at the stares I was getting, I licked my lips. "That was Chris, from my collage. He wants to meet up tomorrow and discuss something." Blushing at the ring tone, not what I was saying. Raven's eyes flickered with jealousy.

"At Porchino's?"

"Yes, at Porchino's. It's his favorite restaurant." Taking another bite of my pie.

"It's also a reserves only restaurant. So, he had to know you'd say yes to going in order to get reserves." Raven took a drink, his hint stinging me.

"Raven, there is nothing intimate with me and Chris. We're just friends." Raven nodded his head.

"The ring tone says otherwise." My eyebrows rose.

"I happen to like Casual Sex." My mother coughed. "It's a good song. If you think for a second Chris is going to try something, you can order me not to go. You are my master after all." With that, I threw my napkin to the table and left the room. Chris was a friend. He wouldn't do anything. He just needed to discuss something with me. Besides, Chris had a girl. But I wasn't going to keep defending myself in a battle that Raven was obviously sure he'd win.

Refusing to see any of my family off, I sulked well into the evening, keeping my door locked and only leaving when I needed the bathroom. At about eleven o'clock, I headed into the bathroom to prepare my bath. Stopping short, the bath water was already drawn, and Raven was sitting in the tub waiting for me.

"Raya, we need to talk." He started. I turned to leave to find the door locked.

"Micha! Let me out! I don't want to be alone with Raven." I pounded on the door. Micha giggled from the other side.

"Sorry, sis. Raven wants time with you. Have a nice bath." I heard her footsteps pad down the hall.

"Raya, please join me." I turned around to look at Raven. I knew I could trust him. I wasn't sure I could trust myself.

"Fine, but I'm not getting undressed with you looking at me." Raven nodded his head, closing his eyes.

"There. I can't see a thing now. I won't open them til you're in the water." Slowly stripping, I kept my eyes on him. He never peaked. Quickly slipping into the bubble bath he had prepared, he opened his eyes.

"What do you want to talk about?" I swallowed, refusing to look at him.

"For starters, this Chris guy." I rolled my eyes.

"For god's sake, Raven! The guy is a friend from collage! He's got a girl, and he was never interested in me." This seemed to put Raven's nerves to rest a bit.

"That's good to know. Thank you for putting me at ease. Just remember, if he isn't human, he can steal you from me if you kiss him." Rolling my eyes again.

"I know. As far as I'm aware, he's human. At least, he doesn't feel like anything but human." I popped one of the big bubbles to my left.

"About the song that's his ring tone." I laughed.

"That's the male ring tone I use. If it's a guy, it's their ring tone. Save for my dad. He's a different song."

"I would hope so." Raven chuckled as he touched my arm. I jumped slightly. I didn't realize he had gotten closer to me. "I won't hurt you, Raya." Raven's voice was soft as his lips brushed my ear. A shiver shot through me, and I turned to look up at him.

"Raven." I whispered.

"Hm?" He nuzzled against my cheek, tilting my head just enough to kiss me. Returning the kiss in full, his hand moved from my chin down to my neck, caressing me.

"We aren't talking much." I whimpered against his lips.

"No we aren't." His smile against my mouth was intoxicating as his hand slipped further, cupping my breast, gently massaging it. Inhaling sharply, I pulled away slightly.

"You wanted to talk. Kissing is not talking." Raven cleared his throat, as if fighting the urge to take me again.

"You're right. What do you want to talk about?" I shrugged.

"You were the one that wanted to talk. You tell me."
He shrugged.

"We discussed what I wanted to talk about." "Oh."
He chuckled again. "Well, what did my mother say
before she left?"

"She said I passed." He changed positions so that my
back was against his chest, one hand across my belly, his
other still cupping my breast. I nodded my head.

"Do you know what she meant by that?" He shook
his head. "She meant you have her approval for being
my . . . master." I couldn't tell him it was for a husband.

"I see. I'm glad she approves. Now, I just need the
approval of one other person." He sounded distant. I
knew he meant me, but I wasn't ready to give it.

"I can't. Not yet." I whispered. He squeezed my
breast lightly.

"I'm fine with waiting, Raya. I'm not going to force
you into something you're not ready for. Just know that
I'm here, and waiting for you." I nodded my head.

"Thank you, Raven. Now, about this job I'm
supposedly going to be starting?" Raven chuckled.

"I see Micha told you about it. Very well, I'll tell you.
You'll be designing your own line." My heart skipped a
beat, my head twisting to look at him.

"You mean it?" He nodded, smiling.

"Thank you!" I threw myself into his chest for a hug,
knocking us out of the actual tub onto the rim which
could be used as a seat. I could feel the heat coming off
of him, his manhood semi-firm against my belly.

"You're welcome, Raya." He smiled at me, then he
went still and got a serious look on his face.

"What is it Raven?" I asked.

"Raya, love, if you don't get off me, I can't guarantee you'll remain untouched much longer." My eyes widened and I jumped off him, climbing out of the tub all together. Grabbing a towel and quickly wrapping it around myself, I went to the door. Finding that at some point, Micha had unlocked it, I stepped out and into my room. Quickly drying myself off, and putting on a silk tank and sleep sorts, I turned to find Raven there with just a towel around his waist.

"Yes?" He came towards me, a mischievous glint in his eyes.

"I came for my good night kiss." He wrapped his arms around me, placing them firmly on my lower backside, grinding me against him. Swallowing, I licked my lips. I wanted to jump him. I really and truly did. But, I wasn't going to. I didn't want to seem that weak. I would get to know him, live with him awhile. He bent down, kissing me deeply on the lips. I parted my lips slightly, and his tongue invaded almost instantly, teasing and caressing every corner of my mouth. A whimper escaped my throat as my legs started to turn to jelly. His growl echoing my own noise, pulling me harder against him to keep me standing.

Breaking the kiss, gasping for air, his mouth went to my neck. Nipping it and kissing it so tenderly and sensually that my eyes rolled back in my head from the pure pleasure I was feeling. Coming back to my senses, I pushed against him, breaking his hold. Gasping at my desires, I looked up at him.

"I can't yet. I'm sorry Raven." He smiled at me, nodding his head.

"I understand. Just know one thing, Raya. By the next full moon, you and I will lye together in the moonlight.

You're losing the battle within yourself to resist. I admire your fight, but you've nothing to lose, and only things to gain." He walked to the door, and shut it softly behind him. Throwing myself to the bed, I fought the urge to pleasure myself. I was aching for him. My entire body wanted it. I wasn't ready, and yet, I suddenly didn't think I really cared if I was or not. I wanted it. I wanted him. Raven was right. I smiled to myself. The next full moon, I promised myself as I drifted off into a steamy dream.

Chapter 4

Turning sideways and looking at myself in the mirror. I was getting ready for dinner with my friend, Chris, at Porchino's Authentic Italian Restaurant. It was this big, fancy, reserves only restaurant. I decided to wear something that I had worked on, finishing it just before my interview with fate. It was a dress that was meant to look a bit like a sari, but instead of the separate top and bottom to a sari, this one was one piece with jeweled chain connecting the top and bottom in complex patterns. The top was off the shoulder, and the over lay wasn't present. It was a deep midnight blue with silver chains with onyx for gems. The slit on one side went all the way up my hip. My midnight blue stiletto sandals completed the outfit.

Raven whistled from my door, making me jump. I hadn't known he was there.

"Wow. Now that's an outfit." He walked towards me, motioning for me to turn for him to see the whole thing. Doing so, he had a smile on his face when I turned back to face him. "Very beautiful. Is this from your collection?" I blushed at his compliment.

"Yes. I hadn't gotten a chance to take photos of this particular piece, so it's not in my portfolio yet. However, I do have a black, gold, and red version of it also done, and ready for photos. I thought the blue was the better option for tonight." He nodded his approval.

"Very much so. Brings out the blue in you eyes." I blushed again. "I wish it were me taking you, I have to say. I am jealous." Rolling my eyes and grabbing my purse.

"Thanks, Raven. I promise you can take me out somewhere fancy next time. Chris just wants to talk, and Porchino's is his favorite location."

"He's got deep pockets. I believe the cheapest item on the menu there is about twenty dollars at dinner time." I nodded my head.

"He does indeed." The door bell rang. "That will be him. So, I should be going." I stepped past Raven just as I heard Micha open the door, and greeting a familiar male voice.

Walking downstairs slowly, I got a good view of Chris. He was a looker too. His semi-short blonde hair had been swept back, held in place with styling gel, his eyes the shade of charcoal which matched his suite for the evening perfectly. When his eyes fell on me, he stopped and stared for a bit.

"Chris, you're staring." I smiled at him. It seemed to shake him out of the daze he was in.

"Good god, Raya! If I'd known you were gonna be this drop dead gorgeous, I would have called the family mortician to have a spot set up for me! Damn woman! You grew up." Laughing and punching him in the arm.

"Don't give me that Chris. I'm hardly something to compare to Bethany." Chris' smile faded as he rubbed his arm.

"Yeah, well, we should get going." He turned to Raven and extended a hand. "Don't worry, I'll have her back by nine. Ten at the latest." Raven shook his hand.

"Do see that you do." Raven wanted to kill him, I could tell that. He wouldn't because I wasn't in danger. That didn't stop him from wishing he could. I ushered Chris out the door. When we got to the car, he opened my door for me. He was being a proper gentlemen. After getting in, and starting the car, he broke the silence.

"Bethany and I broke it off. I wasn't going to say anything before dinner, but her family wanted either a ring or it to end. She ended it because she wasn't ready for that kind of commitment." I was stunned. All throughout middle school, Bethany and Chris were an item. Chris was the captain of the football team, and Bethany held cheerleader captain the whole time. Now, after most of their life, they weren't an item.

"I'm so sorry Chris. I didn't know. I wouldn't have made that joke if I had." He waved it off.

"It's not a problem. I feel free. I can have as many female friends as I want, and not have them be closet friends anymore." I nodded my head, the car ride drifting into silence for the rest of the trip to the restaurant.

Reaching the restaurant, Chris and I were led to a candle lit table way in the back. Our waiter showed up shortly afterward. The walls of the restaurant were an off white with painted ivy growing up them. Potted ivy hung in some places as it grew over the lattice fencing that was part of the ceiling. The floor was made of terra-cotta stones and live musicians played at some tables upon request.

"Yes, we'd like a bottle of your finest red wine for a start." Chris smiled at the man.

"Most certainly." He quickly left us with our menus.

"See anything you like, Raya?" Chris smiled at me over his menu.

"Hmm. I'm thinking about either the seafood scampi or the chicken Parmesan."

"Both options are quite tasty. I've had both."

"Which would you suggest?" I smiled at Chris.

"Ah, you want me to order for you, knowing you the way I do." I laughed.

"Pretty much, Chris." The waiter returned with a bottle of Pinot Grigio. Pouring a bit in a couple of glasses, and handing one to each of us. Sampling the wine, Chris and I agreed on it, and he poured us full glasses.

"What can I get you to eat?" The waiter smiled at us.

"We'd like an order of the stuffed mushrooms for start. We'd also like two chicken Parmesan dinners." Chris handed both our menus back to the waiter.

"Of course sir. I'll get your appetizer out to you in just a minute and make sure they put these orders in right away." He quickly left our table again.

"Ok, Chris, you owe me an explanation."

"I do?" Chris looked at me as if I'd shocked him as he took a sip of his wine.

"Yes you do. What's going on?" Chris smiled.

"I felt like taking my favorite female friend out to a wonderful dinner." I rolled my eyes.

"Don't give me that. You said over the phone you wanted to discuss business." Chris sighed.

"Raya, can't we leave business to be discussed over dinner? Or after dinner?" I pursed my lips.

"I suppose. Can you at least give me a hint?" Chris nodded his head.

"I suppose I could. Tell you what, it has to do with your career field, and my money." I snorted.

"That's not much of a hint, Chris." The waiter brought us the mushrooms, and quickly left again. Taking one and popping it in my mouth, my eyes closed as the silkiness of the mushroom melt in my mouth.

"I know. So, here's another hint. It has to deal with Milan." My eyes popped open, and I coughed slightly, taking a drink of my wine.

"Milan?! You want me to do a showcase at Milan?!?" Chris smiled.

"See, this is why I didn't want you to know before dinner." Chris chuckled as dinner arrived.

"Oh look, dinner. I can't believe you're asking me to show in Milan." Chris smiled as he finished his bite.

"I'm not just asking about Milan. It's Europe's fashion week next month, and I'd like to show you all week. It's wonderful exposure, and I know you'll have a blast doing it."

"Oh you bet I'd have a blast! Just think, to have my designs backed by you, Christino Forgioni, would be amazing." I took a long drink of my wine.

"That's good. There's just one other thing, and I'm not sure how you'll react to it." I put my glass down.

"What's that?" Chris took a deep breath.

"I would like you to come to the family reunion that will also be taking place that week, in Sicily, as my date." I slowly finished my bite, and took a drink of my wine.

"So, let me get this straight, in addition to me being your showcase at the Europe fashion week, you also want me to go to your family reunion in Sicily, pretending to be your girlfriend?"

"Yes, that about sums it up." Chris licked his lips.

"Chris, if your family is expecting Bethany, and you show up with me, where does that leave me?" Chris sighed.

"Look, I've already told them I'd be bringing someone with me. A friend from school, not Bethany. They don't expect anything from you." I perked an eyebrow.

"Really? Can you honestly tell me your family won't protest that we aren't engaged?" Chris cringed.

"No, not all of them. But they'll understand." I put my hand up to stop him.

"Chris, I am not comfortable going to your family reunion as your date since we aren't dating." Chris pulled out a red velvet box from his pocket, and pushed it towards me.

"Open it." I took the box, and opened it. Sitting inside the box was a ring made of white gold with sapphires, white and pink diamonds in the design of orchids. The sight of the ring took my breath away.

"Chris, what is this?" I looked up from the ring to Chris. Chris cleared his throat.

"Raya, I know I dated Bethany a really long time. Long enough to know she wasn't the right woman for me. I've done plenty of soul searching since we broke it off, and the one thing I'm sure of, is that there has only ever been one person in my life that has always had my back. Always made me feel special. That one person has been there from the time I stepped off that bus for the first time in middle school, to the time where my family became one of the most important members of society of our time. That person, Raya, is you. I've never had to pretend to be someone I'm not when I'm with you. I know now, that I was the biggest idiot in the world, the Veil included, for ever asking Bethany to go out with me, when my one true girl was there the whole time. Which is why, Raya Misten, it would do me the most wonderful honor in the world, if you would be my wife." I stopped breathing. I couldn't tell if my heart had stopped as well.

"Chris . . . I don't know what to say. You blindsided me with this that's for sure." Chris nodded his head.

"Yes, I realize that, and I should have done something sooner, but I couldn't think about anything but you being by my side." I looked back at the ring, thinking hard for a minute. Did I like Chris? Yes. Was I attracted to Chris? Yes, but not the same way I was when I was in school with him. Did I want to marry Chris? No. I wasn't ready for a commitment like that with anyone. Not Raven, and sure as hell not Chris. I licked my lips, even bit the bottom one. How to tell him no, gently? There was no way.

"Chris, I'm really thankfully that you think of me in such a strong way, and Milan would be amazing. But, I can't. I'm sorry, but I can't. I'm not ready for such a commitment." Chris hung his head, and chuckled lightly.

"Yeah, I understand."

"Chris, I really do mean it." Chris waved a hand, got the bill, paid, and helped me to my feet and out of the restaurant. Inside the car, the start of the drive was silent. I knew Chris was angry, and I didn't blame him.

"Chris, I am really-"

"Just don't Raya." I flinched.

"Chris, I-"

"God Raya! Do you ever think about someone other than yourself?" Chris raged.

"What do you mean?"

"Gee Raya, I take you out to a fancy dinner, give you a ring that cost almost forty thousand, and you throw it all back in my face, not thinking about my feelings or what I want." I blinked at this accusation.

"Well, Chris, if you had asked me first, I would have told you ahead of time that I wasn't interested."

"Don't give me that bullshit. You enjoy having men spend thousands of dollars on you, only to throw it back in there faces."

"Bullshit! I have never given you an inclination to think I'm ready for a relationship!" Chris slammed on the brakes, veering off the road. Getting out of the car and coming over to the passenger's side, he ripped open the door, and ripped me out of the seat, slapping me across the face in the process.

"Raya, you're a real bitch. You need a man to teach you a lesson." Dazed slightly, Chris hit me again and again. After the forth or fifth hit, I hit back, catching Chris off balance enough to struggle free.

"You need to leave me alone now." I backed away from Chris, trying to ignore the stinging of my jaw.

"You Bitch!" Chris charged at me. I barely moved out of the way.

"RAVEN!" I cried out. A flutter of feathers appeared, Raven in the middle of them.

"Raya what is going on?" Raven stepped closer to me, seeing my face, and touching it softly. Raven's eyes turned murderous. He wheeled around to see Chris staring at them.

"You did this to Raya?" Raven growled at Chris, not really asking a question and taking a step forward.

"It's your fault! You took her from me!" Chris yelled at Raven.

Raven moved so quickly I couldn't keep up with him. After a few minutes, and plenty of screams from Chris, Raven stopped. He was holding a very bloody Chris up by his neck.

"No, Chris, this is your fault. You made me hurt you because you hurt my Raya. Now, you can die like the dog you are." With that, Raven threw him into the side of his car. Walking towards me, he bent over, picking me up, and holding me close to him, and disappeared into the night.

Chapter 5

Getting me back home, Raven took all the precautions possible to ensure that I wasn't in pain. Shortly after Raven and I were inside the house, Micha rushed to our side, helping with getting me undressed and in the bath.

"What happened?" Raven asked, sinking in next to me, Micha joining on the other side. I choked back a sob.

"He bombarded me. He took me to Porchino's, offered to endorse me as a showcase for Europe fashion week, then he tells me if I say yes, he wants me to go to his family's reunion. The next thing I know, he's handing me a ring and asked me to marry him." Raven growled in his throat. Micha hushed him.

"Then what happened?"

"I told him I wasn't ready for a commitment of that kind. He said he understood in the restaurant. Then, after we left, he blew up at me. Accusing me of taking advantage of him and his money, then throwing it back in his face." Micha held me close to her.

"I should have killed him." Raven's face went to one of pure rage.

"No, Raven. I should have listened to you. I shouldn't have gone out with Chris. I didn't know how he was. We never actually dated before . . ." Raven twitched.

"Why haven't you dated before?"

"Because he had a girlfriend from middle school and up. Hang on! Let me call her. She might be able to tell me something about Chris." I went to grab the phone, but Raven was faster, handing it to me, making me sit back again. "Thank you." I said to Raven, as she punched in Bethany's number. After three rings a woman answered the phone.

"Hello?"

"Hi, Mrs. Smith? It's Raya, Raya Misten. I was wondering if I could talk to Bethany?" A choking sound came from the other end of the phone.

"I'm sorry, Raya. I know you were good friends with Bethany. But, she's dead."

"What? When? How?" I sat upright in the tub.

"She was beat to death by that bastard."

"Who?"

"Chris! Who else?!" With that, the phone call ended. I ended my end of the call, handing the phone back to Raven, lying back against the tub, stunned.

"Well, what happened to Bethany?" Micha asked.

"She said Bethany's dead. Chris beat her to death." My voice faltered. Micha fell silent. Raven seethed.

"Why hasn't he been charged?" He raged.

"Because of who he is." I whispered.

"And who the bloody hell is he?" Raven roared, making both Micha and I jump.

"He's Christino Forgioni, heir to the Forgioni empire." Raven and Micha inhaled sharply.

"That explains a lot. The Forgioni's are the ones who let us know where Tęmina is being held. They pay for it." Raven crossed his arms. I shuddered.

"Would that mean he'd be at Tęmina?" Raven uncrossed his arms, wrapping them around me.

"Of course not. Unless you're taking part, you're not welcome." Micha nodded her head.

"That's right." I relaxed.

"Alright. I think I'm done." I shifted over Raven, who held his breath as my chest caressed his. I climbed out of the tub, wrapped a towel around myself, and headed into my room. After I left the room, Raven let out his breath.

"God, how do I resist the temptation?" Micha giggled, climbing on top of Raven.

"Because I keep you in check." She whispered as she started teasing his mouth and neck.

I woke up early the following morning, finding myself the be the only one up, and started making coffee and breakfast. Pancakes, eggs, toast, sausage, and bacon. Not long after I started working on the bacon, Raven's arms wrapped around me, kissing my neck lightly.

"Good morning, love." He whispered in my ear.

"Morning, Raven. Did you and Micha have a good time in my bathtub last night?" Raven winced.

"Yes, we did. It would have been better if you had stayed." Raven cupped my breast, massaging it lightly. I bit my lip.

"Raven, if you don't stop . . . . Oh god . . . ." Raven chuckled in my ear.

"If I don't stop?" He prodded, playing with the other breast as well.

"I'm going to burn breakfast . . ." I almost moaned.

"Party pooper." Raven let go of me, and went to the fridge, pulling out the orange juice, taking a big swig from the carton. Micha cleared her voice from the doorway.

"Please, don't let me interrupt your fun." She strolled into the kitchen, and plopped down in a chair, getting her plate full of food.

"We were already done." I finished off the bacon, joining Micha at the table.

"Oh sweetheart, you hadn't even started yet. Raven would never be done that quickly." Raven choked on his coffee. "Even his quickies are at least an hour long." My eyes bulged out of my head, and I slowly turned to look at Raven, who had just joined us at the table.

"Really, Raven? Your quickies are an hour long?" I was blushing, and I knew it. Raven set his coffee cup down before answering me.

"Raya, love, I am a healthy young man. I would think that an hour long quickie for me is rather short. If you like, when we do engage in our coupling, I can take all day and night, and still make you see the stars for the first time." I hadn't thought I could go any more red, but by the time Raven was done talking, I thought my ears had burned off. Micha cackled in glee at seeing just how de-virginized my ears were becoming. Clearing my throat, and changing the subject.

"So, when do I start work at your company?" Raven finished the rest of his breakfast before responding.

"Next week. I would have had you starting sooner, but I've got nothing but meetings for the rest of the week, and I wanted to personally make sure your workspace was set up properly." Nodding my head.

"Alright. That should give me time to start planning my next project." Taking the plates and putting them in the sink, Micha and Raven got up. Micha started saying her morning goodbyes, Raven politely saying he couldn't stay and skip the meeting. She eventually dropped it.

"Raya, I'll be seeing you later." Raven wrapped his arms around me, kissing my neck. I twisted to face Raven, kissing him deeply. Raven growled low in his voice, and picked me up, placing me on the table behind him. "Raya, if we don't stop, I won't be going to work today." He moaned against my lips. I released him from my hold, kiss and all.

"We wouldn't want you to miss any important meetings now would we?" I giggled. Minor payback for burning my ears off. Raven growled in his throat at me.

"Minx. Do that again, and I will be having me some cherry pie right here on the table." My eyes widened, and I blushed deep crimson red. With Raven having the last laugh, he left for work.

Several hours after his meetings were done for the day, Raven was about ready to head home, when his secretary called him.

"Yes, Abby?"

"Sir, there's a man here to see you. He says he's your brother." She said, uneasily. Raven swore.

"Alright, show him in."

"Yes sir." She hung up. A few seconds later, Cain walked into his office.

"What do you want?" Raven stood, putting his hands in his pockets.

"Dear brother. I came to apologize for my intrusion at your house the other night." Cain sat in the chair across from Raven's desk.

"Oh really? That's unusual for you." Raven leaned against the window behind his desk.

"Yes, I know. That's not the only reason I came."

"I figured as much."

"Are you aware that Ţemina is almost upon us?" Raven stiffened.

"Yes. Why?" Cain sat forward in his chair.

"Are you going?"

"I haven't decided yet." Cain sat back, a smile on his face.

"I see. You do remember what father said right?" Raven's jaw clenched.

"Yes."

"So, you'll be going right? I'd hate to take the family house from you without a fighting chance." Raven reeled on Cain.

"You will not have that house! Not so long as I'm alive!" Raven was shouting at Cain now.

"Ah, good. Then I'll see you at Ţemina." Cain rose from his chair.

"You can believe it. I'll be there." Raven slammed back into his chair.

"Good. See to bringing that new slave of yours with you. I would love to sample such a lovely one." Cain laughed as he left the building. Raven cursed him out of the building. Micha and Raya would not be happy. He grabbed his jacket, and headed home.

Raven slammed the door to the house shut when he got home.

"Micha! Raya!" He yelled. Micha came running from the upstairs.

"What has you in such a mood?" She asked, crossing her arms

"Where's Raya?" Raven threw his jacket on the couch. Micha bent over to pick it up and hang it on the coat hanger.

"She's not home right this second." Raven wheeled around to her.

"What? Where the hell is she?" Micha turned on her heel, facing Raven.

"What is wrong? You're upset, and I don't understand why." Micha crossed her arms again.

"My brother came to my office today. He's made the Tęmina open season for him to try for you and Raya." Micha stopped dead where she was.

"WHAT?!" Raven nodded his head.

"That's right. That's why I need Raya here. I need to make sure she understands." Raven dropped onto the couch.

"Raya's at the store. She's buying some new fabric for her new project. I gave her her new credit card, and she was gone." Raven barked out a laugh.

"She's like you were at first, Micha. Give her a credit card, and see how fast she runs it up."

"That hurts, Raven."

"Aw hell. I'm sorry, Micha. I didn't mean to hurt your feelings." Raven grabbed her as she was passing by, making her fall on top of him.

"Make love to me right here, right now, and I'll forgive you." Raven laughed.

"Of course, Micha." Kissing her deeply, neither noticed the door opening.

"Oh god! Get a room!" My voice caused both Micha and Raven to jolt upright.

"Raya!" Raven jumped off the couch. Catching me by the waist, and raising me in a twirl. After setting me back down, he gave me a huge kiss.

"Raven, stop." I pushed on Raven lightly.

"Sorry, Raya. I was worried about you." I rolled my eyes as I headed to the stairs.

"And when is that not something new?"

"When Cain declares open season on you and Micha." I stopped halfway up the stairs.

"What do you mean?" I came back down the stairs.

"Cain has brought up something our father had declared. If either of us does not attend the Tęmina, we lose our nobility title, and the one that did go, takes the slaves that belong to the other, as well as the family house." My eyebrows perked.

"What happens if both of you show?" Raven smiled.

"I keep the house, as I'm the oldest, and we both retain our titles and slaves." I nodded my head.

"Ok . . . Do I have perform as well? Or can just you and Micha do that?" Raven's smile faded.

"Unfortunately, we would all have to perform." I nodded my head.

"I won't go."

"Raya, what are you thinking? If you don't go, I'll lose you." Raven stormed up to me.

"Raven I can't. I'm not ready!" Raven cursed.

"Dammit Raya, I would never force you. But I don't have the luxury of waiting. Tęmina is only a few short weeks away." I crossed my arms.

"You can force me if you need to, Raven. But I will never love you. Nor will I go to you willingly if you do.

I. Am. Not. Ready." I ground out, and stormed upstairs. Raven stared after me for a few seconds, cursed under his breath, then turned on Micha.

"Micha, you know how I am." Micha nodded her head. "You have two weeks to prepare her for Tęmina. I'd hate even worse to make it be her first time, but by God I will not lose both of you just because my second slave is being selfish and not understanding the rules of the world she is now part of." With that, Raven stormed out of the house. Micha headed upstairs. Reaching my room, she knocked on the door.

"Raya, sweetheart, it's Micha. Can I come in?"

"The door's open." Micha entered the room.

"Sweetheart, we need to talk . . ." Micha went into the room, and shut the door behind her.

Chapter 6

The next couple of weeks pasted by in a blur. Before I had even realized it, it was the end of the time Raven had given Micha to make me prepared for my first time. Rushing back home after work, I entered the house without paying much attention to the interior of the living room. The lights were off, and the fireplace was light. Upstairs in my room, there were candles everywhere, and rose petals on my bed. Doing a double take at my bed, I stopped short, blinking. Heading back downstairs, I walked through the living room again. Sure enough, I hadn't mistaken the fireplace going.

"Micha?" I called, heading into the kitchen. First thing I noticed was a candle lit dinner set for two, and someone coming up from the wine cellar. Raven appeared, dressed in a deep blue silk shirt and black pants. He smiled at me.

"Micha won't be joining us tonight, Raya. I asked her to see to some of the details at my family estate. Please, join me for dinner." Raven smiled, setting the bottle on the table and getting out a couple of glasses.

"Let me go change I suppose." Raven nodded his head.

"Please, feel free to." I nodded, and headed back upstairs. I shut my door, my mind racing to escape. I knew I couldn't. Raven would find me. I'd put up with dinner. But, I would not do anything more. I changed from my work suit, putting on a navy blue dress that faded into a deep purple. The jeweled collar to it clasped shut around my neck, the slit on the right side when all the way to my hip. Checking my appearance one last time, I opened the door, and slowly shut it behind me. Walking back downstairs and into the kitchen.

"Ok, Raven. I'm ready for dinner." I swallowed as Raven looked me up and down very slowly, as if mentally undressing me, a smile slowly forming on his face.

"You look very elegant, Raya." I smiled back at Raven.

"Thank you, Raven." He pulled out my chair out, and scooted it back in after I sat down. "Thank you again."

"Of course." Raven sat down. Conversation during dinner was pretty non existent.

"How was your day at work?" Raven asked after a bit.

"Good. I had some minor issues with the pattern of one of the fabrics, but I'm sure it'll work out."

"I see. I'm sorry to hear that." I shrugged.

"It's fine. I'll figure something out." Raven nodded. Dinner went on without much more conversation. After dinner, Raven took the dishes away, and brought out dessert. Cherry pie. I laughed, much to Raven's confusion.

"Sorry, I just can't help it. A few weeks ago, you told me we'd have cherry pie if I kissed you again the way

I did. And now, look, we're having cherry pie." Raven laughed too.

"Yes, I suppose we are. That was unintentionally planned." Raven cut both of us a slice, and took his seat across from me. The unease broken by my comment over dessert.

After we finished dessert, Raven escorted me upstairs, to a candle lit bathroom, with a bubble bath already drawn. Raven shut the door behind us, and lightly caressed my shoulders, kissing my neck lightly. I inhaled sharply, as Raven undid the clasp that held my dress up. After my dress fell to the floor, Raven turned me to him slowly. I licked my lips, refusing to look up at him. Raven lifted my face to look at him, and kissed me lightly on the lips. Slowly, he started to unbutton his shirt. I took that movement to quickly get in the bath, uneasy at being in such an intimate situation with Raven. I'd been in similar situations with him, but Micha had always been in the house with us. Shortly afterward, Raven slipped into the bath with me, putting his arm around me, pulling me tight against him. I swallowed. I wasn't entirely comfortable.

"Raya, I love you. You know that, right?" I slowly nodded my head. "Then you know, I would never do anything to hurt you. Everything I do, I do to protect you." Raven's voice was in a calm, hushed tone, his hand caressing my backside.

"I know." I whispered.

"Raya, love, please look up at me." My gaze met his, and I licked my lips. Raven's eyes watched my tongue as it traced my lips. Slowly, he lowered his mouth to mine, pressing ever so slightly. My hand slipped to Raven's neck, holding his head to mine. A moan escaped his throat as he pulled me closer to him. I whimpered into his mouth. Raven's control snapped. In a heartbeat, he had me pinned against the tub wall, caressing me with one hand, the other keeping our mouths connected, grinding himself against my womanhood. Gasping at Raven's loss of control, his tongue traced back down my neck to my earlobe.

"Oh God." I whimpered. My noise seemed to set Raven off even further. He bit my earlobe, causing me to cry out again, his mouth tracing kisses down to my left breast. Kissing it lightly, he took the whole of my mound in his mouth, sucking quickly and roughly. My cries got more intense, each time he sucked on my breast. Raven's other hand slipped between my legs, easily finding the heat of my mound. Rubbing me intensely, my cries intensified to almost screams as my body arched in my own climax. Once my climax started, Raven slipped a finger inside me, quickly finding my g-spot, sending me over even faster than before.

Raven released me almost instantly when my climax ended, still holding me close to him, while I caught my breath.

"That was amazing, and yet, cruel." I commented when I felt I could talk again. Raven chuckled.

"Please elaborate."

"Well, you've pleasured me. But, you haven't had a release." I looked him in the eyes, my hands on his chest.

"Ah, and I suppose you're volunteering, love?" I blushed at Raven's teasing.

"Well, I'm not experienced or anything like Micha is . . . but . . . I . . ." Raven hugged me close.

"Raya, I promise you, I won't do anything to hurt you. I don't care about experience. As long as it's you wanting to do it, I won't stop you." I nodded my head, my hand slipping below the water, taking him firmly, but gently in my hand. Raven inhaled sharply at the sensation of my hand. Ever so slowly, I began stroking it. His body came to life instantly, forcing him to grab the tub to keep from grabbing me. I watched his expressions as I worked, his eyes swiftly rolling back, his moans turning into low, animalistic sounds. Soon, he started to thrust his hips as I stroked, his whole body arching in absolute pleasure. My eyes were wide, watching Raven. Suddenly, he stopped, and I stopped stroking as well.

"Raya, love, you sure know how to give a man a hand job. Regardless of what you think, that was better than anything Micha has ever been able to do." I blushed, turning away from Raven. His hand caught my chin, turning me back to look at him.

"Raya, I love you. I always will. And frankly, if you can flip my switch that easily right now, I can't wait to see how well you can flip it later on." My blush deepened. Raven swept me up in his arms as he climbed out of the tub. Taking me across the hall to my room, he placed me gently on the bed, climbing onto of me.

Kissing me gently, and deeply, Raven's hands caressed my body thoroughly, leaving me almost breathless. His mouth lowered to my chest, taking my right breast in his mouth, teasing it the same as he had the other. Moaning in pleasure, my body arched against his, dragging his attention from my breast to my lower pleasure point. Looking up at me and smiling, he quickly took my mound in his mouth, the sensation flipping a switch almost instantly causing me to cry out.

"OH GOD! RAVEN!" My scream flipping his again, he began ravaging my mound, causing me to buck wildly. Timing it just right, Raven reared up, piercing me fully in one swift thrust.

"God, Raya!" His voice getting my attention, my eyes snapped to him, slowly lowering to where our hips met.

"Raven." My voice a mix between a whimper and a moan, as Raven started to slowly thrust into me. The sensation being so new to me that it swiftly drove me over the edge, my climax stronger than before. Raven, trying to hold on a little longer, lost it as my body contracted from my orgasm, causing him to reach his limit.

"Raya, love, I can't . . . Oh god!" Raven's body pinned me to the bed as his seed spilled deep inside me, both our bodies shuddering in absolute pleasure. Raven rolled off me, keeping his arm wrapped around me protectively. I shifted so I could look at Raven, and smiled at him.

"So much for being able to go all day and night." Raven threw his head back laughing so hard his entire body shook with it.

"Raya, love, we haven't even started yet. The day's still young." He kissed me, and got up off the bed.

"Where are you going?" He turned back to me, smiling the whole time.

"I want some pie. Would you like some pie?" I giggled.

"No, I'm good." Raven disappeared, returning shortly afterward, with the remaining pie.

"I don't see any plates, so how do you intend to eat it?" Raven chuckled.

"How indeed." Raven pushed me against the bed, and started scooping the pie on my chest and belly.

"Raven, what are you doing?" I looked at him, my eyebrow perked at his motions. He smiled as he put the pie down on the night stand next to me. Leaning next to me so that his mouth was inches from mine.

"I'm having desert." With that, he lowered his head over some of the pie, and started eating it off me. The sensation was odd at first, then turned to almost tickling me. When he looked up at me from the top of his eyes, he took not just a cherry, but also my nipple in his mouth, sucking on it, rolling his tongue over it to be sure he thoroughly cleaned it. Gasping at the way he was teasing me, I grabbed the bedding to keep from arching in pleasure. Raven continued to eat the pie slowly off me, my gasps and moans clearing affecting him. Once he had me fully "devoured" he slowly slid inside me again, moaning at my wetness.

"Raya, I don't know how I stopped myself from ravaging you the first night we met. I wanted to so badly." He moaned against my neck, his manhood slowly thrusting deep and sharp into me, making me gasp with each thrust.

"Oh god, Raven. I can't . . . Please . . ." My mind wouldn't form full sentences. Raven chuckled at my loss of words.

"Please, what?" He nuzzled my ear, licking it slowly.

"Oh god. Raven . . . Please . . . more!" My body arching against him. I felt Raven smile against my ear, as he pulled out, then swiftly rammed himself deep inside me. Crying out in surprise at his new found force, he grinned, repeating the swift motion. My arms wrapped around his back, clawing him in complete surrender. Raven growled at the pain I caused his back, whipping around so that I was on top of him, his arms moving my hips on him, pounding me hard and deeper than before. My cries grew more wild by the second, as my orgasm rocked my body again. Our breathing had gotten more intense as he continued pumping into me. My orgasm hit my body, clenching tight onto his manhood. His hands gripped me hard, clawing me in return. Once it ran it's course, I collapsed, feeling the warmth of Raven's seed spilling inside me again. I smiled against his chest, as I looked up at him. The glow of his eyes fading as his breathing returned to normal. He smiled back at me, rubbing my backside.

"Your eyes are so beautiful when they glow." My face flushed a bit, rethinking just what we finished doing that caused them to glow.

"Thank you. I don't think I can go another round, Raven." He chuckled.

"We'll take a five minute breather." My giggle sounded more like a gasp.

"Raven, I mean it, I can't go another round." I smiled at him, enjoying his teasing, until a thought crossed my mind, I jolted up right, biting my lip. "Raven?" Raven tilted his head a bit, a grin on his face.

"Yes?" His hands caressed my back, going around to my breasts, teasing them.

"What if I get pregnant?" Raven stopped teasing me, and pulled me back against him.

"You won't." He held me close.

"But, today, it wasn't a safe day. I could get pregnant." Raven kissed my forehead lightly.

"No, Raya, you can't. A master, or mistress, can't get a slave pregnant, and a slave can't get their master, or mistress, pregnant. The only time either can get pregnant is at Ţemina." His voice soothed my worries instantly.

"I see. So, will Micha and I get pregnant at Tẹmina?" Raven chuckled.

"Only if the three of us decide we're ready for children in our house. That's the way it works, if a slave, master, or mistress, desire to get pregnant, everyone that will be participating in that party must agree to it. So, if Micha wanted to get pregnant, you and I would have to agree that she could."

"Why is it so complex to get pregnant?" Raven chuckled.

"Because the elders of the Veil decided that we didn't need to breed like rabbits. Before that law was written, we were constantly getting women pregnant. We're always fertile, so it's impossible for a woman to sleep with us and not conceive. So, the elders decided we needed to learn to take responsibility for the children we sired, since many were left abandoned. That's how Tẹmina came to be." Raven concluded his history lesson.

"Oh. So, we can have all the unprotected sex we want, and neither Micha or I will become pregnant unless it's at Tẹmina, and only then if we all agree to it."

"Correct." I nodded my head, thinking slowly.

"Raven?"

"Hm?"

"I wanna have a baby with you." The words tumbled out of my mouth before I had fully finished my thought. The look on Raven's face was one of pure shock. I blushed at his look, not fulling looking into his eyes. Raven licked his lips, smirked, then thrust into me quickly forcing out a gasp. "Raven!" He sat up and continued thrusting into me, sharp and deep, my gasps loud in the room.

"If you want a baby, Raya, we better get plenty of practice in." He whispered into my ear, his words making me swoon.

After that, we didn't talk anymore. The only noises coming from us were ones of pure pleasure and ecstasy. I don't know when Micha came home. We certainly didn't notice her at first. It wasn't until she shrieked that we noticed her. Raven and I both turned to look at her.

"Hi, sis." I waved at her from where I was. Raven looked in her direction, his eyes unfocused as he vaguely waved at her.

"Wow, you guys have been busy little hamsters while I've been gone. The whole house reeks of sex." Micha giggled at us. Raven took that point to collapse next to me, barely able to look up at her from the other side of me.

"Sorry Micha. We were making up for lost time." Micha perked an eyebrow.

"Oh, I don't doubt it. Well, in any case, you both need to eat something." We both started to get up. "After you two have bathed of course. Raven, you're not going to bathe with Raya. She needs a break from your relentless sex drive." Micha smiled, which faded after Raven shook his head.

"No Micha, Raya doesn't need a break. I do." I giggled, getting a wide eyed look from her.

"You've run him ragged?" She pointedly asked me.

"Yes, and it's been deliriously fun." My breath wispy and almost song-like.

After we both had thoroughly cleaned up, the three of us met downstairs for some dinner. Conversation was mostly non-existent, until Raven cleared his throat.

"So, Micha. Raya and I talked earlier." Micha perked an eyebrow.

"You mean you actually had a conversation at some point during your frenzy?" My face went deep crimson, Raven smiled as he continued.

"Yes, and Raya decided she would like a baby. So, my question to you, is are you ok with us having a baby?" Micha looked taken aback, and a flicker of hurt shown in her eyes.

"I thought you didn't want children. That's what you told me when I asked about having a baby." My eyes widened as I looked at Raven, who flinched and cleared his throat again.

"Yes, I did say that when you asked. However, since I know you have been wanting one, and Raya wants one as well, I've changed my mind on the subject of children. It could be nice to have little feet in the house." Micha's face brightened up instantly.

"Then yes, by all means, we can have babies this year." I didn't miss the 'we' in her sentence, and neither did Raven, who just nodded his head in acknowledgment.

"Then it's settled. We'll have children this year at Tęmina." A loud cheer went up between Micha and I, as Raven tried to keep our noise out of his ears. "Please, loves, I have a really bad headache. Something about being fucked ragged."

Chapter 7

When Raven, Micha, and I arrived at Tęmina, it was like a whole new world before my eyes. There were strobe lights going, and loud music blaring through the high dollar speaker systems, with a live DJ there. Couches, beds, tables, and pillow piles covered the floor. Bolts of sheer fabric hung from the ceilings, interwoven together to form semi private rooms where masters and slaves could get it on in a little more privacy. The whole place screamed sex rave party to me, not what I would have expected Tęmina to be like. Tęmina, I had been informed, was a week long get together. A party of sorts. A very risque party.

Raven had chosen our outfits for us for this. Micha was wearing a white and neon purple latex catsuit that exposed both her breasts, and all of her lower region. She wore a matching set of latex boots that went all the way up her legs, stopping about four inches from her hips. A matching pair of rabbit ears and tail completed her look. I was wearing a white and hot pink latex catsuit, exposing the same amount as Micha's did, and latex boots that matched hers, but with my color scheme. A set of cat ears and tail completed my look. Of course, Raven looked like he just stepped off a movie scene in his black silk shirt, black leather pants.

"I want my girls to be the center of attention. I want everyone to stop and look at the two most beautiful women that will be there. I want the masters, and mistresses, to wish they had you as their own." Raven had told us while we were dressing.

We stood out, that much was for sure. We were getting the looks he wanted, no doubt about that. Micha seemed to be enjoying the whole thing, waving at people, squealing when she got waved back to. Me on the other hand? I was so embarrassed, I didn't look up. I clung to Raven as tightly as cotton sticks to skin during a downpour.

"Raven?" He turned to look at me, smiling. "I . . ."

"Sissy! You have to look over there!" Micha drowned my voice out, as I looked to where she was pointing, my eyes widening.

"Isn't that Lord Ducunt? He's the Prime Minister!" Sure enough, Lord Ducunt was in a semi-private room with a fairy dominatrix, getting spanked. Raven laughed.

"Yes, Raya, you would be surprised at how many politics are part of our society. Now, what were you going to say?"

"I . . ." My voice was cut short again by a woman approaching us.

"Raven!" She smiled a mile at him, as she finally reached us. Raven looked taken aback, as well as thrilled to see her.

"Iris! I didn't expect to see you here. Are you a mistress? Or a slave?" Raven's eyes trailed up and down her body. She was wearing an ornate silk corset, matching thong, and black latex boots that stopped just above her knees. Iris' hair was black with dark purple streaks in that seemed to almost glow in the lighting. Her eyes were a mix between blue and green, as if they hadn't quite decided on which color they wanted to be. Her skin was fair, not the same shade as mine or Micha's, and she had curves in all the right places.

"I'm a slave. But my master told me to have fun with anyone I wanted. Say, Raven, we never did get to finish our duet last year. So, what do you say? Want to sing with me again this year?" Iris was rubbing her hands up and down her breasts. I knew she didn't want to sing a song I would approve of with Raven. My lips pursed at her intentions, and I hugged tighter to Raven, who glanced down at me.

"Iris, I would love to. However, it's Raya's first time here, and I won't leave her be." I perked up, smiling against Raven's arm. "But, if you want to do a quartet, I certainly wouldn't refuse." My smile disappeared instantly.

"Oh Raven, she'll be fine. Micha will look after her." She pulled slightly on Raven's shirt. My eyes flashed and I was instantly between her and Raven.

"Back off Barbie!" Iris took a step back, staring at me.

"What did you just call me?"

"I'll say it again, in case you're hard of hearing. Back off Barbie!" My eyes started to glow, and I knew it, she backed away for a second before snapping back at me.

"I'm not Barbie! So you take that back, you cow!" I laughed.

"If all you can do is call me a cow, then you've got problems." Raven slapped his hand over my mouth, cutting me off from insulting her further.

"I'm sorry about Raya, Iris. She's new to our world. Of course Micha can look after her, but I'm not leaving either alone this year. A certain someone we both know has made it open season for both of my girls, and I won't risk losing either." Iris nodded her head, obviously calmed down by Raven's words.

"I wish you were my master, Raven. Then we could sing all the time together." Raven chuckled.

"Indeed we could, Iris. Maybe I'll do some trading this year after all." My eyes widened and flicked up to Raven's face. "Of course, as always, my girls won't be up for trade, but I have other things I can tempt your master with." I sighed in relief. Iris nodded her head.

"Alright. I have a favor to ask since it's Raya's first time here." Raven dropped his hand off my mouth, teasing my right breast with it instead.

"And that would be?" Iris put her hand on my leg, slowly slinking it up to my womanhood.

"I'd like to give her a welcome that's fit for royalty." Iris licked her lips, smiling at Raven. My legs started trembling now, they were both teasing me, and it wasn't something I was used to. Raven noticed the change right away, and a slow smile formed.

"Iris, that's a wonderfully generous offer. We'll use a private room though. I think anything more open than that, and Raya might be over stimulated." Iris nodded her head in agreement.

"Right this way then, Raven." Raven, Iris, and Micha practically had to drag me to the room Iris was taking us.

Once inside the room, the door shut, and the room was instantly silent. I took the moments of silence to look around the room. There were mirrors on one wall, with a king sized four poster bed in the center of the room. There were a couple of chairs and couches lining the remaining walls. Raven went over to one of the couches, and sat down in it, crossing his legs. Micha bounced her way over to him as well, and sat down as well. Iris led me to the bed, gently pushing me down onto it.

"Lie back, and just relax. Nobody can come in here now that we're using the room, so no worries." I licked my lips, and situated myself further onto the bed, resting my head in the pillows. The whole thing was comfy.

"Micha." I turned to look at Raven. "Please go help Iris." Micha seemed to be bubbling over with happiness as she got up and came towards me.

Slowly, she unzipped my shoes, and took them off me. After which, she removed the cat ears as well. The bed moved from the other side, and I saw Iris climbing in. Her corset, thong, and boots were gone now, and she smiled playfully at me. Micha got off the bed, after showing Iris how to remove the cat suit the rest of the way.

When Iris got right next to me, she took my left breast in her hand, teasing it light. Biting my lip at first, I didn't understand why she felt the need to do this. Licking her lips again, she squeezed my nipple between her nails, causing me to gasp. Taking that opportunity, she started to kiss me, rolling her tongue back and forth with mine, as if to see what she could get away with. When she finally broke the kiss, I was gasping from pleasure. Her hand slipped between my legs, teasing my mound now. My body arched against hers, as I gasped in pleasure. Her mouth closed around my right nipple as she rolled it with her tongue. Gasping again, my body grew hotter under her. After a minute, she stopped, then looked at me, smiling wickedly.

"Time for the main course." I didn't say anything, just watched her as she moved to where my womanhood was, and licked it.

"Oh god!" My body bucked under her tongue, as she forced me back against the bed, teasing me with her tongue, nipping me lightly, then licking me again. "I . . . I can't . . . take this!" I gasped out as my orgasm hit me full force, my body twitching when it stopped. Iris pulled back, licking her lips.

"For someone who hasn't been here before, you sure are excitable." Her eyes flicked to Raven. "Say, Raven, does she always orgasm when she cums?" Raven smirked, and slowly nodded his head, as her eyes widened. "Really? Wow."

I slowly started to slink away from her, as Raven got up, and removed his shirt, shoes, and pants. I looked at him, as Iris crept closer to him. Raven looked up at me, as he grabbed a fist full of her hair before ramming his cock down her throat. He never took his eyes off me as he fucked her face, or when he came down her throat, or even when he let go of her entirely. The only time he stopped looking at me was when he went back to sitting down on the couch. Iris started to laugh, she was apparently enjoying this.

"Alright, Raven. I get the message. I'll go let my master know you're here, and we'll come by again later tonight." Iris got dressed again, and left the room.

As soon as she was gone, Raven and Micha both were upon me in seconds, teasing me to no ends. By the time Raven was ready to put it in me, I was beyond begging. I couldn't even form sentences. Raven took several turns with Micha and I before we were too tired to fuck anymore, collapsing against the pillows, snuggling together. The last thing I remembered, was hearing him mumble something about little Ravens running around the house.

Several hours later, or at least, I think it was several hours later, a hand touched my backside, waking me instantly. Looking over my shoulder, and expecting to see Iris there, I saw Dratis. Screaming, and jolting upright, waking both Micha and Raven in the process, Iris was laughing at the other end of the room.

"Rise and shine, Raya." She cackled. Raven glared at her, then at Dratis.

"I suppose you're here for the trade you wanted?" He asked pointedly at Dratis.

"Why, yes, Raven, I am." Dratis smiled at us.

"Why, pray tell, can't the trade wait til the end of Temina?" Iris and Dratis both looked at each other then back to Raven.

"Because today is the last day of Temina. You guys fucked, and slept, the rest of the week." Dratis stated. Raven's brow furrowed.

"Don't give me that crap." Iris nodded her head.

"It's true, Raven. Today's the last day." Raven grabbed the clock out from under the bed, and sure enough, it was almost a whole week later. "Well, that's fucked up. Oh well. Food first, trade afterward." Dratis waved his hand at a two whole tables against two walls of nothing but food and drink. Raven, Micha, and I slowly got to our feet, and started a buffet line around the table, only to be joined by Dratis and Iris.

After we had stuffed ourselves to all excess, Raven started the talk of trading.

"Alright, what are you wanting to trade, Dratis?" I continued to enjoy my banana split that I had made, not really caring about the conversation.

"Iris for Raya." I choked slightly on part of my banana. Raven's face went cold.

"My girls are not for trade. You know that." Dratis snickered.

"Relax, Raven. I was just teasing. Besides, you know I prefer men. Iris is the only slave I'm trading. And she's made it clear, she wants you. So, what do you think Iris is worth?" Swallowing my banana, I turned to Micha.

"So, if I'm understanding this right, if Raven and Dratis come to an agreement, Iris is essentially sold to Raven for something in return?" Micha shook her head.

"No, it's more along the lines of the barter system. Dratis has something he wants from Raven, so he's offering Iris in return for what he wants. Raven can then say that he wants something else, or more than just what was originally offered, in return for what Dratis is wanting. Does that help?" I nodded, and Iris giggled.

"Gee, make a girl feel loved why don't you." She stopped when Dratis gave her a look. "Sorry master."

Raven looked over Iris thoroughly before he spoke again.

"Dratis, is she still untouched like she was last year?" My eyes flicked to Iris. There was no way she was a virgin. No way could she be. It wasn't even her first year here. Dratis nodded.

"Yes, Iris is still untouched. Well, except for her back entrance, obviously. I know you took a shine to her last year, but you weren't doing trades, so I couldn't offer her to you then." Raven sat back in his chair, and thought for quite some time before answering.

"I'm willing to give you an hour in the library for Iris. However, if you want longer than that, I have to have something else." Dratis's smile seemed more like an evil smirk.

"Of course, what else would you like in return for, say, four hours?" Raven raised his eyebrows again.

"Four hours huh? Got three other virgins you're willing to part with?" My eyes bulged out of my head.

"Raven, why is the library so hard to gain access to?" Raven sighed before responding.

"The library contains books on magic, mostly the forbidden arts, but magic none the less. I'm in charge of making sure that the people that would want to use the forbidden magic aren't allowed in. However, it's also has plenty on history and the likes, and I know Dratis isn't interested in the magic, so I'm willing to be a bit more lenient with him. Normally, Iris wouldn't be enough for even one hour in the library." I nodded my head, understanding his reasoning.

"Well, I have Randy, of course." My eyes flashed, and apparently glowed, because Dratis sat forward, staring at me for a minute.

"Yes?" I snipped at him.

"Such a beautiful glow." My eyes widened and I averted my gaze back to my sundae. Dratis sat back again.

"But I don't think you want him. What else would you take for four hours?" Raven thought for a minute.

"Virgins, virgins, virgins, and oh yeah, virgins. Sorry Dratis, I won't change my mind." Dratis's mouth twitched.

"Raven, can he have more than two slaves? Is he blue blood?" Glancing at Raven from the corner of my eye, who obviously was thinking about how to phrase his answer. Dratis beat him to it.

"I'm what's known as purple blood. See, there's blue blood, like Raven and Cain; then there's red blood, ones that can only have one slave; and then there's the purple blood. Purple blood gets you some blue blood perks, but otherwise, you're pretty much the same as red blood. I'm allowed up to twenty slaves. Whereas, Raven can have any number he desires. He has no cap on his slaves. I've got nineteen, so I'm pretty much at my cap, which is why I don't mind trading some, that and I know how well Raven treats his slaves, so any I trade him are well taken care of." He turned back to Raven. "I only have four virgin slaves. Iris, Chelsea, Zaila, and Mei Ling." Raven nodded.

"I want to see those other three." Dratis slowly nodded his head, and turned to Iris, who was already getting up and heading out of the room. She returned shortly with three other girls. "When I say your name, step forward so Raven can get a good look at you. Chelsea." The first girl stepped forward. She had fair skin, blonde hair, and emerald green eyes. Raven got up, and started to inspect her as he had with Iris, nodding his head at what he saw.

"Chelsea is it?" He asked her.

"Aye, 'tis my name." Her Scottish accent thick. Raven nodded his head.

"Would you have an issue with being placed under new management?" Raven poised the question like this wasn't the first time he'd been in one of these kinds of deals.

"If my master be wishin' it, then no." Raven nodded his head before turning to look at Dratis.

"That's two." Dratis's wicked smile formed again.

"Zaila." The second girl stepped forward. She was clearly from African descent. Her skin was creamy cocoa, warm chocolate eyes met Raven's, and her curly red hair looked more forced than natural. Raven's brow furrowed a bit as he inspected her, apparently, something about her felt off to him.

"It's Zaila?" Iris giggled, as Zaila slowly shook her head.

"Say zay-I-la." Her voice was just as smooth as her skin, and just as accented as Chelsea's. Raven nodded his head.

"Zaila, can I ask you a question?" I looked up before I had realized it.

"Werewolf." Zaila's gaze landed on me, and she smiled.

"Only half." Raven looked back at me, with his eyebrow raised.

"Sorry. I could smell the wolf. It got stronger when she came closer." Raven nodded his head.

"Well, that takes care of that question. What can you do as a psychic?" Zaila turned to look at him.

"I can shape change into a wolf, for starters, as all half werewolves can do. I can also tell one's future by gazing at the moon with a focus item of theirs. Some hair, or something like that." Raven nodded his head again.

"Last question, would you have an issue with being placed under new management?" He carefully sounded out her name as she had before him, and smiled when he got it right.

"Of course not. If my master wishes it, I would go to the ends of the earth for him." Raven nodded his head as she stepped back.

"That's four." Dratis faked shock as he called the last girl up. "Mei Ling." She was obviously from the Orient. My guess was China. Raven looked her over, as he did the other three. Her skin was the normal creamy Asian coloring, with long silky black hair, and brown eyes to match.

"Mei Ling, correct?" She nodded in response.

"Would you have an issue with being placed under new management?" Raven asked her, and she smiled.

"No, I wouldn't mind." Raven smiled, and she went back to stand with her sisters.

"That's five. Dratis, you'll have five hours in the library on Sunday. So, shall we transfer their ownership now?" Dratis stood up, and extended his hand, which Raven shook with earnest.

"Sure. I'll take Micha and Raya and go get them ready to go. I won't try anything, and you know I won't." Raven stopped for a minute before waving his hand at us to get ready to leave.

After we left, and were on our way to hotel, I turned to Dratis.

"So, how is he going to transfer ownership?" Dratis chuckled.

"He's going to take their virginity. Don't worry, he won't be long. All he has to do is pop a few cherries."

Dratis stopped outside our room, and let us go in, as he stood outside the room, stopping any stragglers from trying to jump us. We finished packing soon enough, and Raven, along with the other four met us not long after that. Raven, Zaila, and Mei Ling got in his car; Micha, Iris, and Chelsea got in Micha's car; and I got in my car. On the way home, I tried to ignore my jealousy that I had. I should be happy for these girls, and Raven. But somehow, I just couldn't do it.

Once we got home, everyone was happy and laughing about something. I quietly made my way to my room instead of joining the others. Shutting the door to my room, I locked it. I knew Micha and Raven would come looking for me, but I didn't want them near me right then. I wanted to be by myself, left alone with my thoughts. Soon enough, Micha was at my door, trying to come in.

"Raya, honey, why won't you come out and get to know your new sisters?" I walked over to the door, pressing my shoulder against it.

"I don't feel well, Micha. I think I'd rather go to bed." Micha didn't say anything after that, but I did hear her head back downstairs. Back towards the roaring of laughter I could still hear. I knew I was being a party pooper, but part me of me really didn't care. I was back to having issues understanding my new lifestyle. Raven could take up a new slave whenever he desired, he didn't have to ask our opinions. It made my blood boil. But, on the bright side, I could go to work tomorrow, and not see them. As long as they weren't models.

It wasn't long after I had sat down at my small work station in my room that another person knocked on my door.

"Yes?" I inwardly sighed, turning to look at my door, knowing they couldn't get in.

"Raya, Raven asked me to come check up on you. Can you please open the door?" Iris.

"I told Micha I was going to go to bed, Iris." I heard her shift outside my door.

"Still, can I please come in and maybe we can talk a bit before you crash?" Shaking my head as I responded to her.

"Sorry, Iris, I'm really not up for it tonight. Maybe tomorrow night." I turned back to cutting the fabric I was working with.

"Well, alright then." Iris sounded truly disappointed, as she headed back downstairs. I sighed again. They were trying to get to know me. I understood, but didn't care. I didn't want to know them. Taking the cutout and pinning it to the mannequin I started cutting out the next piece.

I was halfway done pinning that piece to the mannequin when I heard heavier footsteps coming my way. Raven. Great, I was in trouble, there was no doubt about that. They stopped just outside my room. My eyes flicked to my door.

"Raya." Flinching at the sound of Raven's voice, I didn't respond. "Please open the door." I turned back to my work, ignoring him. I knew it wasn't going to work to ignore him, but I was going to try.

"Raya, I'm not going to ask you again. Now, please open this door." A jolt of electricity went through me. Was that because it sounded more like an order? Shaking my head, I continued my work. I had told him when I first became his slave, ordering me around wasn't going to work for me.

"Raya, open the door. Now." Another jolt of electricity went through me, stronger and more painful than the last. Gasping at it, I shook my head, tears forming in my eyes. I wasn't going to do what he wanted, especially not now that it was an order.

"Raya. Open the god damned door. Now!" The jolt that went through me was so strong, I couldn't help but cry out from it. Getting to the door, and slowly opening it a crack to look out at him.

"What?" I asked, flicking my gaze up at him then back down at the floor. He wasn't mad, he wasn't even irritated. He was pissed.

"Why won't you come down and visit with your new sisters?" I shuffled my foot against the door a bit.

"Because I don't want to. I want to be alone for a little." It wasn't a completely a lie. I did want to be alone. But, the full truth of the matter was I didn't want to be with them.

"Don't lie to me." I flinched at the sound of his voice. "Raya, I've been nothing but honest with you since the very beginning of us. I told you from the get go, you weren't the only one I had. You won't be the only one I'll ever have. I can't guarantee you'll ever be the only one I have. But, I can guarantee that no matter how many other girls I have, you'll always be *my* girl. I will never trade you, I won't remove my mark from you. I'll go to the ends of the earth for you, Raya. And while I do love Micha and Iris both, I would send out an army to search for you. Micha I'd send a platoon, simply because I know what she's been through. As for Iris, I'd call her old haunts. I don't know the other girls well enough to say what I'd do for them." Raven was holding me tight at this point. I didn't recall letting go of the door, but I was suddenly glad I did. "I love you Raya. While I care for Micha and Iris, I *love* you."

It took all my strength to choke back a sob. Raven loves me. *Raven loves me!* The realization of this hit me full force.

"I don't know yet, Raven." I felt him smile.

"Take your time Raya. I won't rush you." He pulled away from me. "Please come down and join us." I turned away from him for a minute, wiping the remnants of tears away.

"Give me a few minutes and I'll be down." Raven walked to my door, slowly shutting it again. After a few seconds, his footsteps faded as he went back downstairs again. I walked over to my bed, and sank onto it.

"Raven loves me." I whispered to myself. I should be happy, but for some reason, I just couldn't. Getting out my cards, I did a quick fortune.

"Anger. Love. Destruction. Wait, that doesn't make sense." I did two more readings, the outcome the same. One reading could be chalked up to the wrong question. Two readings could be chalked up to bad shuffling. Three readings were unheard of, especially with the same cards each time, in the exact same order. "What does the destruction it's foretelling mean?" I muttered to myself, putting the cards away just in time to have Iris burst into the room.

"Come on lazy bones! We've got a party going on downstairs, and everyone in this house is a must attend. So, get up off your butt, and come downstairs and get your party on!" Iris was practically dragging off my bed and out the door. I pulled out of her grasp just shy of my door, forcing myself to laugh.

"I'll be down in a minute. Let me use the bathroom first will ya?" Iris nodded.

"Sure thing, but if you're not downstairs in five, I'm coming back for you." I nodded and shut the door to my bathroom. After I was done in the bathroom, I headed downstairs to find the whole household playing strip poker and drinking. After being dealt in, I knew I was in trouble.

Chapter 8

Horns blared around me as I was stuck in a major traffic jam on my way into the office. I had my designer shades on, despite it being early in the morning. Good old mother dearest wasn't happy when I called to ask about the hang over cure she always used on dad. After listening to her bitch, I had hung up, took a cold shower, downed two pots of coffee, and popped six Aspirin. It didn't work. And now, I was on my way to the office with a killer hang over.

"Come on already! I'm late!" I blared my horn as well, instantly regretting it. This was getting me nowhere fast. "If only the cars would part and let me through." I slumped against my steering wheel, trying to ignore the base drum inside my head. After a few more minutes, the jam fixed itself, and I rushed into work. Raven wanted to see me as soon as I got there.

Rushing into the building, I nearly bowled over someone I'd never seen, or met before. Giving them a rushed apology, I squeezed myself into the elevator just as the doors were closing. Getting out on Raven's floor, and rushing past the receptionist, I stopped short just inside the doors to his office. There was a full fledged conference going on, and everyone turned to stare at me. Licking my lips, my gaze landing on Raven as he slowly stood up.

"Sorry, I'll just leave." I started fumbling with the door.

"Raya, stop. This meeting is about who'll be showing in the upcoming fashion week in Europe." I froze, looking back at Raven. "I called you here, because I wanted you to demonstrate to the board why you're the only candidate in my mind for the job." My eyes widened.

"Raven, is this the reason you wanted me here so early?" Raven chuckled as he nodded his head. "I'm so sorry I'm late. Traffic jam out the wazoo." I composed myself as I headed towards Raven. I had my entire portfolio with me, and I was going to be damned if they were going to tell me no. Getting to the podium he had set up for me, and pulling out the disc, I slipped it into the computer. Pulling up the file, and starting the slide show I had made for this meeting.

"The first few images are the change in style that has been seen over the past five years. As you can see, we've gone from gothic to retro, from boho-chic to everyday casual, and everything in between. I propose to create a new ideal for clothing with my line." Pulling up the slide show of my work. "You'll notice that most of my clothing is based loosely around traditional styles from all over the world. I feel I've modernized these styles, making them my own. I have something fit for every possible situations. Maternity, special occasion, career paths, children, teens, swimwear, and of course casual wear." With that, my slide show ended. "My last few words to you are this. Can I guarantee everyone will love my designs? No, I can't. Can I guarantee they'd sell? No, I can't guarantee that either. What can I guarantee? I can guarantee that regardless of how well my designs sell, I will always keep aspiring to be the best I can. I won't stop just because something I make isn't to everyone's tastes. My goal isn't to be rich. My goal isn't to have my name known throughout the world. Would I like that? Yes, but I don't care about that. What I care about is designing, and enjoying my work. So, if you enjoy doing your job, then you can find it your hearts that I am the right person for the fashion week, and you'll know that I'll work my hardest to sell. Thank you for this once in a lifetime opportunity." With that, I stepped back taking my paperwork with me.

Working in my space, I didn't notice the presence at first. It wasn't Raven's, or Micha's. Standing up fully, I glanced around my office, not finding anything out of the ordinary. Shrugging it off, I went to where I kept the fabric, finding a gold sheer organza, I went back to my bench. Turning around after I was done cutting it, Dratis was behind me, making me scream.

"Sorry, love. Didn't mean to scare you." He smirked.

"Liar. What do you want?" An odd look flashed over his face.

The next thing I knew, my back was against my bench, and he was on me, kissing me hotly. My hand searched for something to get him off me, finding the scissors I'd been using. Grabbing them, I swiftly jammed them deep into his back.

"AARGGH!!" Dratis roared, ripping them out of his back. His eyes flashed as he threw them aside. In the next second he had both my hands above my head, pinned tightly to the bench. "Don't make me angry, love. I will rip you apart."

"Dratis, let me go! Raven will tear you limb from limb if you don't!" Dratis chuckled.

"I don't think Raven will be able to come, love. He's a tad bit busy right now." Fear overtook me entirely now.

"Wh . . . What do you mean?" Dratis laughed again.

"His brother decided to pay him a visit. Cain's contesting Raven's presence at Ţemina, since he never saw Raven there."

"But that's insane! You were there! We were there, you can tell him that." Dratis smirked at me.

"I could, but then I wouldn't get to taste the woman Raven's fallen in love with." Tears stung the back of my eyes. Dratis's eyes followed my tongue when I wet my lips.

"But, you can't. I don't . . . Raven will . . ." Dratis chuckled.

"Admit it, love, you want me to lift your leg and pound your pussy into jelly." A deep crimson blush covered my face as I averted my eyes.

"N-no . . . I—I don't want that." Dratis chuckled again at my stuttering.

"I understand love, really I do." Dratis reached down to his pants, and I heard a zipper. My eyes flashed down at his groin, then back up at him. His smirk made me want to smack him. Grabbing my underwear, he ripped it from my body as he lifted my leg up over his arm, pressing his penis against my slit. Tears started to form at the corners of my eyes.

"Stop this! I mean it!" Dratis's eyes flashed as he swiftly rammed his cock deep inside me.

"AAH!" My whole body arched against his from his entry, my scream bouncing off the walls. Dratis took that as the official acceptance of what he was doing, and continued to force himself deeper and harder into my body. It wasn't long after he started that my mind blanked.

"You're really loving it. I bet you can't get enough of my dick." My eyes rolled to look at him.

"S . . . stop! I . . . can't . . .!" He chuckled before he sped up.

"Don't worry love, I'll make sure to fill you. It's not like you'll get pregnant or anything." My mind snapped back into focus with his statement.

"NO! YOU CAN'T!" I screamed at him.

"Too . . . late!" His hips met mine one last time as he dumped his seed deep inside me. When he was through, he stood there watching me cry. After a few minutes he pulled himself out of me. Putting himself back into his pants, he turned to look at me again. Sitting up, the room was spinning slightly.

"You even so much as think of telling Raven about this, and I'll kill your whole family." My breath stopped as I looked up at him.

"You wouldn't." He smirked at me again.

"Love, I just raped you right under Raven's nose. What the fuck makes you think I won't rape and murder your family? I mean, fuck, love, what are they going to do me? Shoot me? You saw how good stabbing me works. I'd start with the little ones, they're always the tastiest. Then, I'd work my way up to the adults." My eyes widened as he told me how he'd pick off my family members. "If you don't want that, you won't tell Raven. It's simple. You keep your mouth shut, and your family gets to live."

"I . . . I understand. I won't tell Raven." Dratis smirked again.

"Good, love. Now, make yourself presentable. Raven's coming this way." Dratis sauntered off, and I quickly picked up the torn underwear, hiding them as fast as possible. Dratis opened the door, with Raven about to burst into the room. He stopped and gave Dratis a questioning look.

"What are you doing here Dratis?" Dratis smirked.

"Just talking with Raya." Dratis turned to me. "Right Raya?"

"Oh, yes, of course. Just talking." Raven looked at me like he wanted to ask more, but Dratis pushed him out of the way.

"Anyways, Raven, I was leaving. If you're alright with it, I'd like to come over next week for dinner." Raven thought about it for a second.

"Yeah. A weekly family dinner with you is alright." Dratis smirked back at me, with a special look in his eyes that I understood completely.

"See you guys next week then." With that, Dratis left without turning back to us at all. Raven turned to me, noticing the red on my face still.

"Raya, are you alright? You don't have a fever do you?" Raven put his forehead against mine. "No, you don't feel hot." I pulled away from him.

"No, I'm fine. Really. It's just a little hot in here is all." I looked at him, and smiled. Raven nodded.

"Alright, I'll turn up the air." Raven walked over to the thermostat, and adjusted the temperature, and I returned to my work. "Raya?" I turned back to look at him again. In one hand was the bloody scissors, and the other my torn underwear. I went into immediate shock, dropping everything that was in my hands. Raven's eyes went cold, and started to glow.

"Raya, who's blood is on these scissors and why?" I started to shake, Dratis's threat to my family still fresh in my mind.

"I . . . I c-can't tell you." His eyes flashed and his nose flared a bit.

"Don't give me that bullshit! Now who's blood is this?" Flinching against the sound of his voice.

"I can't Raven. I can't." I started to cry. My crying didn't soften Raven's voice like it had in the past.

"Raya, I love you. I always will. I won't hurt you, but you better damn well tell me who the hell this blood belongs to, and now!" The pain from his order coursed through me.

"I can't, god dammit!" I cried as I turned away from him. "He'll kill them!" I felt Raven come closer to me, felt his breath on my neck as he stood right behind me.

"He who?" He hissed into my ear. "Raya, I can't protect you if you don't tell me what's going on." I shook my head. "Did someone rape you?" I flinched, and heard the scissors drop to the floor. Raven stepped back from me for just a moment before twisting me around to look at him.

"You're hurting me!" I sobbed as he pinned me to the bench before ripping my shirt open. My mark was still there, which I had been told once Raven claimed me, it wouldn't go away. Raven gripped my skirt in both hands and tore it open, exposing me fully to him. He stopped, staring at my womanhood for a minute before looking back up at me.

"Raya." I flinched despite his voice being soft and calm now. "God, I'm sorry Raya. I didn't mean to scare you. I . . . I lost my mind when I saw them. I didn't know if you got hurt, or if you fought off an attacker. But, please, Raya, please tell me who it was so I can make him sorry for this." I bit my lip. I wanted to tell him, I really did. *"If you tell Raven, I'll kill your whole family!"* Dratis's voice echoed in my head. Suddenly, a thought came to me. If Raven figures it out on his own, then I didn't tell him, and Dratis couldn't kill them.

"I can't tell you, he threatened my family. However, there might be away around that." Raven perked an eyebrow at me, his eyes still glowed, refusing to move, waiting for me to continue. "See, if you guess who it was, then I didn't technically tell you. Right?" Raven perked the eyebrow.

"Yes, if he specifically stated you couldn't tell, and I guess, then he is bound by our laws to not hurt your family. But of course, that's assuming he's Veilkin." I nodded my head.

"First hint, he's Veilkin."

"You haven't met many male Veilkin. In fact, the only two you know are my brother, and . . . . That bastard! I'll fucking kill Dratis!" Raven got up off Raya, pacing back and forth. "And I just invited him over for weekly dinners."

"He wants me weekly." Raven stopped dead, turning to me.

"As in this day every week, weekly?" I slowly nodded my head, and Raven got a sadistic smile on his face. "Raya, would you be willing to let him attempt to fuck you next week after dinner? Oh, don't worry, he won't get far. I'll make sure of that." He added the last bit when I started to shake my head. Thinking a minute, I shrugged my shoulders.

"I suppose I could . . ." With that, Raven left the room, laughing maniacally.

Exactly one week later, I was in the kitchen preparing dinner for three. Raven had sent my sister slaves to a three day spa resort yesterday.

"I don't understand why I have to cook for him." Talking loud enough for Raven to hear me from the basement. He'd gone down to find a bottle of wine that Dratis would drink.

"Because I thoroughly enjoy your cooking." He came back from the basement and dusted off the bottle he found. "1874. A wonderful year for wine making."

"I see. In any case, dinner will be done in about ten minutes. Shouldn't he be here by now?" As soon as I said that, the doorbell rang.

"Speak of the devil. Go greet him please." Raven smacked my ass as I walked out towards the door. He had me in a micro mini skirt and a halter top. My apron being the only thing I wore that I considered coverage.

I opened the door slowly. Dratis stood there, looking over the porch swing before turning his gaze to me. His eyes flashed the instant he saw my outfit, and he slowly smirked at me.

"Fine evening, isn't it Raya?" I blushed about the same shade as the meat I had just cooked for dinner.

"Yes, it is. Please won't you come in Dratis?" I stepped to the side for him to come into the house.

After he was inside, I went to shut the door, feeling his eyes on me the whole time.

"So, where are we eating?" I turned around to face him again, his eyes glowed with intense lust.

"Since there's only the three of us, we'll be eating in the informal dining room. Please, follow me." I walked around him and headed towards the hallway past the staircase. My stillettos clicking against the wood flooring, making the skirt sway a bit, revealing more than I would have cared for. Dratis whistled low behind me. He was obviously enjoying the view. Once he was seated with Raven at the table, I excused myself.

"So, tell me Raven, how do you keep yourself from jumping Raya's bones when she's dressed like that?" Raven chuckled.

"Self control. That, and she'd beat me if I tried it." I returned to the room at that point with plates and silverware. After placing them, I went back to the kitchen to retrieve dinner.

"I don't know how you manage that. It's gotta be the beating that keeps you in control more." Raven shrugged.

"Maybe you got a point there." Back in the room again, I set the food down and took my spot across from Raven. Now that my apron was gone, Dratis could get a better look at the front of my outfit. My halter top tied only around my neck and bust line, with no real back. The rest of it went down to a few inches above my belly button. The deep v collar made my cleavage even more prominent. My top was an icy blue, my skirt white, and my heels were black. I had even pinned my hair back seductively. All Raven's idea. Which seemed to be working. Dratis couldn't keep but shoot me desiring looks throughout dinner.

Conversation throughout dinner stayed well within business, so I mainly tuned it out. Until Raven and Dratis were looking at me.

"Oh, um, sorry, what did you say?" Dratis perked an eyebrow at me, and Raven chuckled.

"I said, you shocked the board with your speech so much last week, they've decided to accept your challenge. You're going to the Europe's Fashion Week." I blinked, then blinked again.

"Oh wow! That's awesome! I can't wait." I bounced in my seat bit, both sets of eyes flashing as my breasts jiggled and swayed.

"I'm glad you're happy. Micha will of course be going with you, as will four other new models. They'll be your personal models from now on." Nodding my head, before stopping for a minute.

"Who are the other four models, Raven?" He smirked at me.

"You already know them. You might even say they're close as kin." I thought for a second.

"Wait, you don't mean Iris, Chelsea, Zaila, and Mei Ling do you?" Raven laughed, nodding his head.

"Yes, Raya. That would be the four I was talking about." I inwardly groaned.

"Raven, do I have to have them? Can't they be models for some other designer?" Raven stopped laughing, and looked dead at me.

"Raya, my decision is final. Just because they're working with you from now on doesn't mean you mean less. They all wanted to be models, they have the talent for it, and I thought it could be a good way for the six of you to get to know each other and do female bonding." I sat and thought it over for a minute.

"I suppose so. What am I going to do for the men's clothing I design?" Raven shrugged.

"I'll look into finding some male models for you first thing in the morning." I nodded again, turning back to my meal.

After a few more minutes of talk between the big boys, Raven got up. Looking up at him as he showed me the empty bottle.

"I'll be back in just a minute. It seems we've drank the bottle dry." Dratis smirked.

"Indeed we did. Going to get us a fresh one?" Raven nodded.

"Yep. I'll be back in about five minutes. Raya, entertain our guest while I'm gone, will you?" Blushing, I nodded my head as Raven left the room. Once he was out of ear shot, Dratis turned to me.

"You know love, you've got me harder than this here table. Why don't you go under it and take a good look?" Getting down on all fours, I slowly crept under the table. He pulled himself free of his pants, waiting on me to continue. Swallowing, I took him in my hand, rubbing him lightly. He inhaled sharply then looked down at me.

"Use that pretty mouth of yours." Swallowing again, I slowly licked his tip, before taking him in my mouth. "That's a good girl. You're pretty skilled with that mouth of yours. You'll have to go faster if you don't want to be down there when he gets back up here." My eyes widened, as I started to suck on him faster. I really didn't want to be doing this, but Raven knew about him, and he'd fix the problem.

"Good girl. When I cum, you better swallow it all. Wouldn't want Raven to think something happened between us, now would we?" A few seconds later, I heard Raven coming back. Dratis's manhood twitched in my mouth, as he held my head still, his seed pouring down my throat. When he was done, I quickly crawled back out from the table, and sat back down as Raven entered the room.

"So, what did you guys talk about while I was gone?" I looked over at Dratis, who smirked before answering Raven.

"Raya asked me about Veilkin festivals. I told her the few I participated in, but if she wanted a more in depth history of them all, to ask you." Raven looked back at me, and smiled.

"So, you want to know about the festivals? That's good. I'll give you a long winded explanation of them all later." Smiling back at Raven as he sat down.

"Thanks. I'd really appreciate that." Raven smiled as he opened the new bottle.

After dinner Raven was so drunk, Dratis and I had to carry him to the living room couch. After setting him down, I went back to the dining room and cleared the table. Dratis followed me into the kitchen. Grabbing my breasts from behind, he squeezed them.

"Let's you and I go upstairs for some real action, love." He licked my ear, his breath hot against my skin.

"We can't!" Dratis twisted my nipples before answering.

"Don't forget about your family. I've waited all week, like a good little boy. You're going to make me a very bad boy if you don't want them dead." Gasping slightly at both what he said, and what he was doing to me, my gaze went to the living room. "He's out cold. Will be all night long. So, stop worrying about it. A bomb could go off and it won't wake him." He started to pull me towards the stairs, stopping next to the couch.

"Of course, if you'd rather, we can do it right here. Right in front of him." Glancing at Dratis, then back to Raven. Dratis wouldn't. Would he?

Chapter 9

"Tick tock, love. What's it going to be?" Dratis whispered in my ear. My mind was still shocked that he'd even think of doing such a thing. "Time's up." With that, Dratis pulled my top off me, then yanked my skirt up.

"No! Not here!" I hissed at him.

"Too late. You had your chance."

Keeping me pressed hard against him, he released himself from his pants, pressing his hard shaft against my ass. Lifting my leg so that if Raven did wake up, he'd get a perfect view, he plunged his manhood deep inside me. It took all my strength not to scream. Raven had told me Dratis would do this. It was the perfect set up.

"Come on, love. Scream for me. I told you, he's out. Nothing will wake him up now. Or did I not hit your special spot when I entered?" He pulled himself out fully, then rammed back into me.

"Ah!" I couldn't stop myself that time, my whole body twitched with each thrust.

"Oh, so you're *that* kind of girl." Dratis bit my neck before he continued talking. "This'll be real fun."

Pulling himself from me entirely and ramming himself back inside, I cried out again. He repeated this action several more times, the more he did it, the more my mind blanked.

"P-please!" Dratis stopped just outside me.

"Please what, love?" My breathing was shallow, my voice more of a husky whimper.

"P-please . . . g-give . . . me more!" Dratis chuckled.

"What a lovely whore you are. Fine, love, I'll give you exactly what you want." He shoved me down so I could stare directly at Raven's face, as he continued to ravage my body the way he had been. My cries drove Dratis wild as he plunged himself into me nonstop.

Sometime after Dratis put me like this, Raven opened his eyes. I don't know when, I didn't realize he had until I saw him lift an eyebrow and smirk at me.

"Ready, love?" My mind, now halfway back to it's senses, translated what he meant.

"Wait, please! D-don't cum inside me!" Dratis pumped into me one last time as I felt him twitch, followed by warmth.

"Sorry, love. You're body's too much for me not to leave my seed in you." Tears formed in my eyes.

"That's all well and nice, but did you have to fuck right on top of me?" Dratis pulled himself out in a hurry, dropping me on top of Raven, who was now glaring at Dratis, as he backed away. Tripping over the recliner, he fell onto the floor.

"Raven, cousin! You're awake!" Dratis's half smile was one in pure panic. "It was all her fault you know. She was so horny, but you were out cold. What was I supposed to do? I couldn't leave her like that." Raven pulled my hair back with one hand, smiling at me.

"I know you raped her at the office last week, and no, she didn't tell me. I found the scissors with your blood on them." My eyes slowly closed. I couldn't handle anything more. I'd done my part. Raven would take care of Dratis now.

"Raven, I didn't rape her. She was begging me for it. I swear!" Raven's voice was cold.

"Don't take me for an idiot. I knew you'd try something the minute Iris came running at me at Tęmina. But, I thought I'd give you the benefit of the doubt. I thought I could trust you. Apparently, I should have ripped your soul from you back when you tried this with Micha." Raven eased up, holding me carefully as he put me back down on the couch, my eyes opening enough to see him smile at me with soft eyes. He truly did love me. Raven turned back to facing Dratis.

"Hey, look, Raven, I'm sorry. I won't do it again, I swear. I just couldn't help myself. I don't know why. You know I'm into men, not women. There's just something about her that seems to call to me." Raven stopped short as I grabbed his pants leg, forcing him to glance back at me.

"What would you do if I let you live?" Dratis blinked. "Answer me dammit!"

"I'd help you get rid of Cain." Raven took a step back before composing himself again.

"I thought you and my brother were best buddies." Dratis shook his head.

"I like living. There's more fun in living than in death. I'll be your personal spy on him. I forever pledge my allegiance to you, Raven, forever forsaking Cain." Raven seemed to be thinking it over for a second.

"Well, you two are the closest out of all of us. Get over here, and we'll make the blood pact. I'll be damned if you think you'll screw me over." Dratis jumped up, pulled his pants up, taking big steps to get to Raven. I couldn't see what they were doing from my spot here on the couch.

"Ah damn!" Dratis jumped back from Raven a few minutes later. "Fuck! Do you have any idea how much that hurt?" I could see him holding his hand, which now looked charred.

"I guess I don't know the strength of my blood." Raven's voice brimmed with mirth, as he turned back to me.

"I'm not going to kill Dratis. But he won't hurt you, or your family, again. He's bound by the same blood laws that bind us." Raven rubbed my cheek with his thumb.

"What . . . do . . . you . . . mean?" My breathing hadn't quite gone back to normal yet, and Raven smiled at me.

"Dratis has forfeited his power, and become my slave. Yes, masters can fall just as quickly as most rulers, Raya. Dratis can't even talk to you without my permission." I looked over at Dratis, who avoided looking at me entirely. He wasn't happy with his situation.

"What happens to his slaves?" Raven smiled at me again.

"That depends on what I decide. They are now, technically, mine. Think of each master their own country. When another master over powers them, making them their slave, all slaves the newly conquered master has goes to the one that conquered him. As such, I can get keep his slaves; trade them; auction them; or I could just release them from my power. Meaning they'd become lost ones, which is what Micha was when I found her. It's not pretty, but I could do it."

"I . . . see." Dratis still refused to look at me. Raven turned to look back up at him.

"Tell me Cain's current plans." Dratis ran his good hand through his hair before responding.

"He's pissed you have Raya. He's been staying out at Thorncaste, I don't know why, but I know he's been spending tons of his time there." Raven stiffened.

"Thorncaste?! Why would be there? While it's true Father left that estate to him, I didn't think he'd actually use it. What's he planning?" Raven muttered the last bit as if to himself.

"Thorncaste?" Raven glanced at me, sighing before answering.

"Thorncaste is a large castle in the middle what's known as Demon Woods, a forest in the Veil that's feared by even the strongest of Veilkin. Back in my father's rule, he used the castle as a place of terror. He'd take anyone that questioned his rule there, and torture them until they either begged for death, or died all together. It's also where he murdered my mother." I stared at Raven.

"I'm sorry. I didn't know." He shook his head.

"It's nothing to worry about. I don't remember her, so I have no feelings of longing for her. In any case, if he's opening that place back up again, he's got something planned. Dratis, you'll keep to his good side, and find out what it is." Dratis nodded his head, his hand now slightly less charred.

"Then I should be going. Damn, when will my hand heal fully?" Raven smirked.

"Its what you get for messing with Raya. It'll be fine in about an hour. In the meantime, you can keep your slaves. I'll figure out what I'm going to do with them later." Dratis nodded his head, and left the house. After he was gone, Raven turned back to me.

"I hope you're not mad I didn't kill him. I figured he'd be more use to me alive rather than dead." I smiled back at Raven.

"It's fine. I understand." Raven nodded.

"Good. Now, let's get you upstairs." He picked up me, carrying me to my bed. After setting me down, he climbed over me, nuzzling my neck. "Now then, I believe you and I need to have some fun." Giggling as Raven started his teasing of my body.

"I believe so as well."

Chapter 10

Over the next few weeks, Dratis popped in and out giving Raven several reports about Cain's comings and goings. All of which confirmed he was indeed getting Thorncaste ready to be used, but with no idea when that would be, or on whom. One particular day, he appeared in our kitchen cut all to hell. Since I was the only one there at the present moment, I dashed to get the first aid kit, then started tending to his wounds.

"Raven!" I called, knowing he'd come. Shortly after, he did indeed appear before us.

"Raya, what was so . . . Dear gods Dratis! What happened to you?!?" Raven looked over Dratis with a skeptical eye. "Did Cain do this to you?" Dratis shook his head.

"No, some of this is from Raya's patching me up. OUCH! That was a joke, love. You're doing wonders for my ails." Dratis turned back to Raven. "Cain wanted me to test a new toy of his. Of course, when I started to ask him what it did, he went cryptic on me, talking in circles. So, I got the pleasures of being experimented with, and on, and that's why I look like a glorified mummy. OUCH! WOMAN! I told you, I was joking the first time. Glorified mummies hurt when you hit us!"

"And glorified mummies shouldn't make jokes about how a woman with no training is bandaging them up." Dratis flinched.

"Then maybe, love, you should take some lessons. I hear they're free at the fire house." I reached around for the frying pan, when Raven grabbed my hand, shaking his head.

"What's going on in Thorncaste?" Dratis slowly sank further into the chair as he began explaining.

"Well, not much has changed since my last report. Cain's decided to transform the whole place into a torture place. The hallways aren't even safe if you aren't him. He's made the whole place sensitive to his power, and his alone. The one place I've found that doesn't try to disembowl, maim, or kill you is the the main torture room. Although, whatever he's got planned for that room, I haven't a clue. I went in there once to let him know that I was going to go out for a smoke, and he slammed the door in my face. The only other safe, well, semi-safe, places are the bedrooms. Which is nice, since he's gone to living there full time now. If I'm there, and at his side, like most times, he sends a slave through whatever he wants tested. To tell you the truth, Raven, I think the Harvesting needs to wipe that place off the map." Dratis closed his eyes, as Raven slowly sank into a chair.

"I don't think the Harvesting will happen any time soon, Dratis." I looked back and forth between them, without either really noticing.

"Oh, another thing, he's got Drayce and Seirath helping him." Raven froze at the names.

"Um, hello, new person to your world. Who are these Drayce and Seirath people, and what's the Harvesting?" Both men looked at me, as if noticing me for the first time since Dratis started explaining. Raven smiled a bit.

"Well, you know about the Veilkin in the human world. But the truth is, there are seven Veil Kingdoms. Each kingdom is compiled of the one species that is most common in that kingdom. The kings just recently changed, as a matter of fact. I'll try not to lose you in the full explanation. First and foremost, you're aware of four kingdoms. They are: Luciferia, kingdom of the demons; Luniscopia, kingdom of the Lycanthropes, otherwise known as werewolves; Sanquinesia, kingdom of the vampires; and Floriatia, the kingdom of the fairies. Now, along side these four kingdoms, are three that most humans have no idea exist. Those kingdoms are: Avalon, kingdom of the warlocks; Dragonia, kingdom of the dragons; and Atlantis, kingdom of the merfolk. Now, warlocks can blend in with humans no problem, since they were originally humans. No one knows how they came to be a people of the Veil, not even them. Although there are those who would try to tell you differently, Odin, for example, the new king, he claims to know exactly how they came into being. But, the odds of that being true, are next to none. Dragons have no desire to go forth into the human realm, simply because they'd rather not have to flee it again. Knights slaying dragons were real, and it's what forced the dragons into the Veil in the first place. The human world was just too dangerous for them to have children in anymore, so the fled. Lastly, the merfolk don't see the point in showing themselves to the human world. Why should they? They have nothing to gain, and not much to lose for it either. So, they remain in their little kingdom, refusing to show their faces to anyone." I nodded, surprisingly, he didn't lose me.

"Ok, but what about the Harvesting?" Dratis and Raven both looked at each other before Raven cleared his throat and continued.

"The Harvesting, Raya, is something that happens when a kingdom gets too powerful and out of balance with the other kingdoms, or if a kingdom poses an immediate threat to the balance of the Veil. The Harvesting is a creature that's far older than any kingdom in the Veil. There are theories among the warlocks that it was what actually created the world, not just the Veil, but the whole world, and everything in it. We believe the Harvesting to be a black mass of neutral energy. The only time it's even on this world is when it's here to, as we put it, harvest. The black mass slowly devours whatever is inside it. People, cities, land. It doesn't stop, until it's finished collecting whatever it came for. Then, it simply vanishes." I stared at Raven, my face full of skepticism.

"That sounds like a story your parents would tell you to make sure you don't go out at night. An old wives tale." Raven slowly smiled.

"Yes, to an outsider, I'm sure it does. But, it's real. At one point in time, there were nine kingdoms. There was an angel kingdom, and a siren kingdom. Now, there's only the seven." I waved it off.

"That's obviously because a kingdom, or kingdoms, took over the other two." Raven shook his head.

"If that was the case, there would still be angels and sirens in the Veil. But, there isn't. They were all destroyed by the Harvesting." I sighed. There wasn't anything I could say to convince him otherwise.

"Alright, then who's Drayce and Seirath?" Raven looked to Dratis, expecting him to explain, only to find him sound asleep.

"Drayce is the king of the dragons, and Seirath is the king of the demons." I nodded my head before stopping.

"Wait, I thought you were blue blood." Raven flinched.

"I am. Seirath is . . . Seirath is complicated." I shook my head.

"Raven, that's what he is, not who he is." Raven sighed.

"Seirath is-" Raven was cut off by the doorbell. "Saved by the bell." He quickly got up and headed to the door.

"Raven! Long time no see!" A male's voice floated in from the living room, followed by a grunt. I went to the doorway, seeing Raven embraced by a man almost as tall as him with charcoal hair and black eyes, that quickly landed on me. The man tossed Raven aside as he quickly walked towards me.

"I'd heard Raven got himself a woman of beauty unmatched, but I never thought it would be true." A blush crept up on my face.

"Thank you." I whispered, as Raven got to my side, and stuck his hand between us.

"What are you doing here, Seirath?" My eyes widened, as I glanced between Raven and the man, who apparently didn't like being interrupted.

"I should force you to call me Highness. Or Majesty. King. I like King better." Raven's eye twitched. "But I'll be nice to my big brother, and not force you into knowing your place." My eyes widened again.

"Br-brother?!" I choked out, as I backed up looking between the two. There were certainly similar features. Mentally comparing them to Cain, Seirath and Raven did look to be brothers. Cain must have been adopted.

"Yes, Seirath is my little brother, and king of the demons." Raven sighed, as if the position didn't make him happy in the least.

"Aw, you've been talking about me have you?" Seirath gushed.

"I've been getting a lesson on the kingdoms of the Veil." Seirath nodded his head.

"Good. Any sister of mine must know about the history of the Veil." I blushed again. *Sister?*

"Seirath, you still haven't answered my question. Why are you here?" Seirath straightened himself out.

"Because I wanted to share my future bride with my adoring big brother. Or at least, a picture of her." With that, he whipped out a photo of a young girl with iridescent hair and violet eyes. "What do you think? Won't we make a picture perfect couple?" I took the photo from him and stared at it for a second.

"Wait a minute! I know this girl!" Raven glanced at me, as Seirath swooned over my statement.

"Who is she? She looks like a child." Seirath stopped swooning, and grew agitated.

"She's the heiress to the Danno Conglomerate. Her father was killed almost a year ago. But this photo looks to be a couple of years old." Seirath went back to his honey struck face.

"Yeah, but she's still a child. I didn't think my kid brother would be interested in children. Apparently I was wrong." Seirath snatched the photo back.

"How dare you insult my bride! She'll be your queen after all!" Raven straightened up as he went to the fridge.

"She's still just a kid. Doesn't even look to be out of pull ups." He got himself out a beer, then tossed one to Seirath, who caught it easily without looking.

"How dare you! She's going on thirteen! She's already a woman!" He popped the bottle open and drank it in one gulp. Raven slowly popped open his, and took a swig of it.

"Maybe. But when she becomes the queen of Luciferia, I'll be there as her loyal servant. Just like the rest of my family. But, until then, don't get your hopes up that this child-bride of yours will become your queen." Seirath waved his had at Raven's words.

"Of course she'll choose me. I'm the best looking king, the strongest, the most devious, and of course, the most sensational lover of them all." I perked an eyebrow at him. He was full of himself. Yep, definitely related to Raven.

"How do you know you're the most sensational lover?" I asked, getting a snicker from Dratis. Turning to look at him, he dipped his head as his shoulders shook with the uncontrollable laughter as he was trying to keep quite. Shaking my head and turning back to look at Seirath. His face was only a few inches from mine, causing me to shriek and jump back a bit. Raven turned to see why I shrieked, only to stop dead in his tracks. Seirath cupped my chin and held my face so he could get a good look at me, a slow grin forming on his face.

"Raya, dear sweet sister, I'd be more than happy to satisfy you if Raven is incapable of doing so." My face turned hot, my eyes flicking back and forth between him and Raven. Would Raven say anything? Seirath was his little brother, but also his king.

"Seirath . . ." Raven started towards us, before Seirath turned his gaze on Raven. Raven stopped dead in his tracks. "Bastard! Release me!" Seirath's smirk grew wider.

"I don't think so, Raven. While you are my brother, I am your king. If I want to have some fun with my sister, then I will. Afterall, it's not like you're formally married to her. You've only claimed her. That's completely different than marriage." Seirath taunted.

"Dammit, Seirath! You have a bride! Leave Raya alone!" Raven all but roared at him. Seirath pulled me against him, pinning me tight against his body.

"What can you possibly do to stop me Raven? I have all the power in this situation. Had you taken the throne, as your right, you would have the power to stop me. As it is, I'm the king. Without the power to command my subjects, you'd easily over power me. However, you refused the throne. You didn't want the responsibility that came with being king. I'm the second strongest demon in all our kingdom. Second, only to you, dear brother. But, when you denounced the throne, it went to me. I took it gladly, since it came with so many perks. I could easily kill you with just a little command." The look on Raven's face was one of pure fury. "If I wanted to take Raya from you, I could. I have the power to remove your mark from her entirely. Our grandfather used to have a harem. I could always bring back the old ways. Kumiko could be my main queen. Raya, dear sweet Raya, could easily be the first of the many in my harem." Seirath looked down at me. While he had a smile on his face, I knew instantly he was dead serious.

"Seirath, you can't take her!" Raven ground out. Seirath kept his gaze on me.

"Oh? Who would stop me? You, big brother? You can't even move unless I allow it. Dratis? He's your slave, and bound by your order not to approach Raya unless she asks him to. However, even if she did ask for his assistance, he's still a demon. I can easily prevent him from moving like I did with you."

"Seirath, father made you swear not to change the laws of one wife!" Raven sounded like he was pleading with Seirath, who waved off his words.

"Enough time has passed since I've been king. I can easily restore the old ways without getting any question from anyone. No, if I wanted to take Raya as my own, there would be nothing to stop me. Not you, not Dratis. Not even Cain would be able to prevent me from taking her. All it takes, is one little kiss." Seirath pulled my shirt down far enough for Raven's mark to be visible, and dipped his head to it. Pushing against him as hard as I could, his hot breath right above the mark telling me just how serious he was.

"You can't have me! I'm Raven's!" I tried to push harder, but to no avail. I felt his lips form a smile against my skin.

"You're only Raven's so long as you bear his mark. After you've been claimed, the only way to transfer ownership is to kiss the mark. This destroys the bond between master and slave, forging a new bond between the one kissed and the kisser." His tongue trailed his lips as looked up at me. "I truly desire to mark you. I don't understand the desire you cast over me. It's like you have a pheromone that only Veilkin can sense. It makes me wonder." Seirath placed his lips against my skin, just above Raven's mark, barely missing it. Gasping at the heat of his lips, my mind blanked.

"Makes . . . makes you wonder what?" I tried to force out words, to keep me in the here and now. I shouldn't be like this. He wasn't Raven. Seirath opened his mouth, letting his tongue trail little circles up my chest and neck. Stopping only when he reached my ear.

"Makes me wonder what Ambrosia tastes like." My heart stopped. Ambrosia was the nectar of the gods in Greek mythology. Seirath was comparing me to Ambrosia? How could I taste anything like that?

"Please . . . Seirath . . ." My mind was blanking again.

"Please what, Raya?" His voice was husky. All I could hear was my heartbeat and his breathing. It was like the whole world didn't exist.

"Please . . . I can't . . ." I felt him smile against my ear.

"Of course, Raya." His head dipped back towards the mark.

"RAYA!" I heard Raven's voice boom in my head, drawing me back to my senses.

"NO!" I shoved against Seirath with all my strength, breaking from of his grasp. Grabbing a hold of the kitchen sink to steady myself as I caught my breath. When I felt a little steadier, I looked back at Seirath. "No. I won't be yours. I won't let you have your way with me. I belong to Raven. Marriage or not, I bear his mark. I carry his child. I will not be yours, now or ever Seirath." My voice was steady. Seirath's face darkened instantly after I finished my bit.

"A pity, Raya. I could have spared you. Oh well. I suppose you'll learn the error of your ways soon enough. Until next time, dear brother." With that, Seirath took his leave. As soon as Seirath left, Raven rushed to my side, holding me close.

"I'm sorry, Raya. I didn't know he would do that. Please, forgive me." I held Raven tight.

"There's nothing to forgive." Despite what I said, the back of my mind replayed Seirath's words. He could have spared me, and I'd learn the error of my ways soon enough. What did he mean by that?

Chapter 11

"Come on, we need to get everything loaded. If we don't hurry, we might not make it to the opening ceremony!" I directed the moving crew as they sped up their work with getting all the equipment we would need at the Milan Fashion Week showcase. We were running behind by twenty minutes, and we had a plane to catch.

"Calm down, sis. Before you have a coronary." Micha laughed as I glared at her.

"Maybe you can be calm, after all, all you have to do is show up and get dressed up. I, on the other hand, have to work my butt off to make sure everything makes it there." She laughed again.

"That's why I'm riding with you, sis. Raven specifically asked that I ride with you to help you keep calm." I nodded my head.

"Alright. I appreciate that." Raven came out of the building and walked up to us.

"Raya, Micha, I won't be able travel with you. I have to head to Milan in just a few minutes. I wish I could travel with you both, but I have to take care of our arrangements." I nodded, smirking as I grabbed his tie and pulled him closer.

"You better be ready for us when we get there." I whispered in his ear before kissing him on the lips. Letting him go shortly after the kiss, he straightened himself out and smiled at us.

"Of course I will be. See you both later." He kissed Micha, then went to our new sisters and gave them the news. Once they had said their good-byes he walked past us again, muttering as if to himself. "If these women don't kill me, it'll be a miracle."

After another twenty minutes, everything was loaded up, and we were on our way. Micha and I were in my brand new black Barracuda with bubblegum pink interior. I still loved Raven's reaction when I told him what kind of car I wanted. He'd laughed and said not in a million years. But, sure enough, three days later, I got my Barracuda.

"I want to go over the routine one more time with you Micha, then I'll get on the phone with Iris and Randy, and we'll go over their parts again. I want this to be perfect." Micha laughed.

"Aye aye, captain. I start us off with one of your stunning casual wear dresses, followed by Iris in a shirt and pants, Chelsea follows her in a tank and shorts, she's followed by Zaila in one of your masterful boho-chic skirts and off-shoulder long-sleeved tops, and she's followed by Mei Ling in one of the short skirts and Asian inspired tops. After that, the boys come out in their casual wear. Once that's done, we all come back out, in the same lineup, in swimwear, followed by formal wear. And the grand finally is the wedding, where you'll be the bride, and we'll be the bridal party. The only thing I don't know on that one, is who your groom is supposed to be." Micha perked an eyebrow at me, and I blushed.

"It's Raven. He finally gave me his answer last second." Micha squealed with glee.

"I *can't* wait to see him in that tux!!" I grinned.

"Neither can I." I called over to Iris's car to make sure she knew the routine, which they all assisted with stating, followed by a call over to Randy's car.

"Yeah, we know." He confirmed, rattling off the same information.

"Good, I want this to be perfect. No screw ups! I mean it Randy." Randy's voice turned sarcastic before Dratis could take the phone from him.

"Yes, princess, we know exactly how you want this done. You don't need to worry about us messing things up for you. We wouldn't dare. Afterall, we're your slaves now. We do as our mistress commands, without fail, or we answer to Raven." I nodded, before realizing they couldn't see me nod.

"Yes, that's right. You better not forget what got you to your position either." Dratis chuckled.

"Oh, I'm not likely to ever forget, love. Personally, if I thought for a second I'd walk away from it alive, I'd do you all over again." I stiffened slightly.

"You hadn't better even think about it, Dratis. You're already in deep—AHH!" The rest of my response was cut off as we were hit from the side by something I didn't see. My last few conscious seconds were of hearing Dratis' voice yelling into the phone by my ear, and seeing a vaguely familiar head of charcoal hair and black eyes.

"Sleep Raya, the pain will stop when you sleep." And the world slowly faded away from me.

Raven sat down at the airport, waiting for his flight to board when his cell started to ring. Glancing at the number, he answered with an annoyed sigh.

"Yes Dratis?"

"RavenRaya'sgone!   She'snotansweringherphone, neitherisMicha. Somethinghappened, I heard them scream, but then I lost contact with them." Raven stiffened in his seat as he slowly sat forward.

"Calm down, Dratis, you're not making any sense. Take a deep breath, and repeat what you just told me." Dratis took several deep breaths before he repeated himself.

"Raya's gone. She's not answering her phone, and neither is Micha. Something happened to them. I heard them scream, but then I lost all contact with them." A knot tightened in the pit of Raven's stomach. Someone had taken Raya and Micha. Only one possible person came to Raven's mind.

"Cain."